{ twolonelyheavens }

A STUDY IN HUMAN OBSOLENCE

Written By

Steph Cai

Special Thanks

Lemy

Aria

Marisa

reaper ☆

{ twolonelyheavens }
A STUDY IN HUMAN OBSOLENCE

ISBN: 978-0-646-74015-7

A catalogue record for this book is available from the National Library of Australia.

Cover illustration by Raiden Phillips
Cover illustration assist by Clovis Wong

Published by Steph Cai from Perth, Western Australia

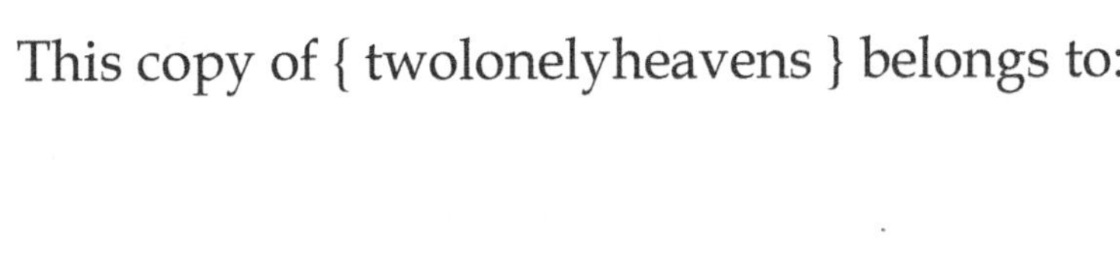

This copy of { twolonelyheavens } belongs to:

Hi, my name's Steph. Thanks for picking up my book. I'm glad the cover caught your eye. It was drawn by my very talented friend, Lemy with assistance from reaper.

This is my debut. I'm an independent author, and I wrote this with my friends by my side. I taught myself book distribution to stay independent, and getting an ISBN was such a hurdle that my friends even helped fund it (thank you again, Lemy, Aria, and Marisa).

You likely found this at a secondhand bookstore after I donated it. Why do I work so hard to distribute it myself? Because I love my friends; they are my family. As much as I wrote this for myself, I wrote it for the people *like* them.

I wrote this for the people who are tired of performing a version of themselves that doesn't fit. It's for those who feel lost in the process of becoming who they were meant to be, and the weight of what that means to the people around them. I see a lot of people out in the world navigating that shift, just like my friends. Or maybe, that person is you.

All I ask is that this story reaches the people who need it, and that they find something beautiful in these pages. If you know someone who would like this book, reach out and I'll try to get a copy to them.

If you want to talk to me about anything at all, criticism, appreciation, or even a single typo, I would love to hear from you at:

twolonelyheavens@proton.me

If you think what you have to say isn't important enough to email about, I'd love to hear why you feel that way. Thanks for reading; I hope you enjoy the book.

Prologue

Chapters I - III

CHAPTER

I

New Territory

The frost bites upon contact.

The air is razor thin, tasting of crushed ice, high-altitude ozone, and the faint mist of burning cedar. Tightly packed snow compresses with a dry crunch, fracturing into glitter across the pavement. Massive, multistorey chalets rise from the snowbanks, their dark, polished mahogany beams leaking condensation against thick panes of heated glass. The wind funnels through the steep, jagged peaks of the Alps, carrying the sharp sting of the fresh winter down into the blinding white luxury of Verbier.

Train doors hiss open, spilling stale heated air into the

frost. Koa hits the pavement first, his teeth tearing through the foil of a granola bar, taking a large bite of processed oats. Beside him, Minty shifts her frame, pressing her hooves into the pristine snowpack with a quiet crunch. Her thin winter coat offers little resistance to the biting wind, the light fabric snapping against her sides, while her skirt flutters around her knees, exposing her furred legs to the sudden chill. Ery lingers on the transport step, her feathery antennae furling forwards, twitching as they filter the sharp downdraft. Jules steps out last, her sneakers meeting the frost. She pushes her cloudy glasses up the bridge of her nose, her rigid shoulders dropping as she watches the three of them absorb the unfamiliar world.

She smiles gently.

A pair of heavy mahogany doors parts, flooding the group with a rush of warmth from a lobby of polished oak and roaring hearths. The air is thick with the scent of dried vanilla and expensive leather. Koa and Minty are agape at the sight of the pristine architecture, whilst Ery is mildly impressed, and Jules looks indifferent.

A receptionist stands rigid behind a long, sprawling desk, offering a smile as Jules approaches. "Welcome, Ms. Sterling," the receptionist says, sliding a silver keycard across the smooth grain. "Your all-inclusive premium suite has been paid in full. I hope you enjoy your stay."

She pushes a thin, cream-coloured receipt forward. Koa watches her take it with a subtle nod, his gaze snagging on the final digits printed on the bottom of the slip. The granola bar in his hand crumbles slightly under the sudden pressure of his grip. He quickly glances between Ery and Minty, the rigidity in his shoulders snapping the cardigan tight against his frame. "Did… did either of you see that?" he whispers, his voice pulling thin against the quiet jazz humming overhead.

Minty's ears twitch, her eyes darting between Koa's expression and the receipt disappearing into Jules's pocket. Her tail, previously swaying, drops down, her fingers clenching the flimsy lapels of her thin coat against the sudden influx of unquantifiable value. The heat of the lobby suddenly feels intimidating. Ery, tapping a nearby dark wooden pillar, tilts her head slightly towards Jules.

"I wasn't aware you were a Sterling," Ery murmurs, her breathy tone blending into the ambient noise. Jules's hand slips out of her pocket, her knuckles brushing against the seam of her trousers. "I don't think about them too much, for obvious reasons."

Koa jogs into the centre of the living space, his shoulders corded tight under the strain of his three oversized duffel bags. He lets them hit the wide central plush rug with a leaden thud. Jules kneels beside her sleek, hard-shell suitcase, pulling the zipper in a smooth line. From the front pocket, her fingers pinch a frayed, dog-eared magazine clipping.

The glossy finish has long since rubbed away, leaving the image of the Les Attelas outlook dull. Koa hovers over her shoulder, wiping a sheen of sweat from his forehead with the sleeve of his cardigan. "Damn! Is that an antique?" he chirps. Jules rests her thumbs against the whitened creases, flattening the frail paper against her knee. Her gaze lifts from the clipping, watching Ery draw a shape on the frosted windowpanes and Minty carefully aligning her hooves between the rug's woven patterns.

"I cut this out when I was fourteen," she says, returning the slip of paper back into the front pocket.

"I didn't have a good reason to go until this year."

Jules immediately sweeps her hand back into her bag, her expression hardening into a sharp focus. The snap of the metal ring-binder pings across the room as she pulls out a thick, laminated and colour-coded itinerary, the pages hefty with dense, calculated blocks of text. She stands up straight and clears her throat, catching everyone's attention. Minty's ears flicker at her expression, realizing she's about to begin. "The gondola departs at 1400. That gives us exactly eighty-four minutes for thermal outfitting, food, and transit. Any questions?"

The group herds out of the heated pine, down into the biting, high-altitude downdraft of the valley. The descent into the village is a crash of friction and noise.

Snow glare reflects off luxury storefronts, mixing with the chatter of thick winter coats brushing past one another and the heavy scent of roasted almonds and scented sugar.

They all press into a high-end thermal outfitter, the narrow aisles towering with displays of thick leather, hanging fluffy coats and polished steel. Minty's hooves click unevenly against the polished hardwood floor. She tucks her elbows tight against her ribs, her long tail pressed flush to her hind to squeeze through the racks.

A subtle shift in her weight nudges her against a freestanding display of winter boots, sending the stand rumbling. The metal legs screech against the floorboards for a second before swaying nervously and settling back into stillness. Over the racks at the other side of the store, a man with a pristine groomed beard peeks over at the commotion.

Eyes darting between him and the stand, she ducks her head, her breath fragmenting into short, ragged gasps. "I-I'm so sorry!" She blurts out, Koa, Ery and Jules watching her as she scrambles through her pockets searching for some form of compensation she doesn't possess. Jules steps directly into her space, her fingers clamping firmly over Minty's shaking wrists. "Minty, you can drop the coins. The boots are fine." Minty looks up at Jules, then pans her vision to the boots, which remain in visually pristine condition. "I'm sorry, boots…" She mumbles.

Half an hour later, they step back into the cobblestone, a slick sheen of sweat already coating the back of Koa's neck after he strategically stole the load of every shopping bag. The braided handles of six overloaded shopping bags full of blankets, coats, pastries, and tools dig into his palms, pairs of stiff winter boots clamped awkwardly under his chin. Minty steps lightly to his side, her soft fluff brushing the edge of his collar. She extends a hand towards the heaviest parcel swinging against his knee. "Would you like-" Koa instantly jerks his hip away, the bags shuffling against each other. "What, you think I can't handle… *huff* a little shopping?" He pants, a rigid smile across his flushed face. Jules turns to look at him, squinting. "Koa, how are you sweating?"

Jules's focus snaps from Koa's flushed face to the empty cobblestone beside him. Her gaze darts down the narrow, crowded street, her hands instantly patting the rigid edges of her itinerary. The dense sea of winter wear parts around the clatter of a passing transport, revealing nothing but the stark village square. She swallows and spins around the other way, looking over the continuous waves of other tourists in coats streaming in and out of stores. "Ery," she breathes, before shoving the itinerary into Minty's chest, sprinting, boots crunching against the snow back the way she came.

Minty and Koa are left standing in the middle of the pathway, Koa shuffling his posture slightly under the weight of the bags.

The smell of caramel and hot yeast hits her as she rounds a sharp, shadowed corner behind the bakeries exhaust vents. Ery is crouched low against the frosted cobblestones. The feathery tufts of her antennae curve out. A patch of untouched snow powder gleams beside her, reflecting the sharp, blinding sunlight in a crystalline pattern. Her hands rest limply on the knees of her skirt, the rhythmic rise and fall of her breathing unbothered by the implosion of Jules's schedule two streets away. Jules's boots skid to a harsh stop, her jaw tight as she marches down the alley. Ery's eyes flick towards Jules, who stands above her.

Ery's shoulders are completely unspooled, her teardrop-shaped wings draped loosely across the snow, divorced from the pressure and noises of the village. Jules's breathing catches. She exhales a long, shivering breath of frosted air, her tense posture loosening under the quiet of the alley. Ery rises slowly with a soft smile, stepping into Jules's space and wrapping her thick wing across her shivering shoulder. The soft fluff of her cheek brushes against Jules's temple. Jules closes her eyes, burying her nose into the crook of Ery's neck, the gentle scent of almond milk and cardamom seeping into her lungs.

A vibration buzzes against Jules's ribs, fracturing the quiet of the alley. She opens her eyes, the clatter of the ski village slowly bleeding back into her periphery. Reluctantly pulling back from the insulating heat of the wing, she slides her smartphone from her coat pocket. The digits of the lock screen reflect against the lenses of her glasses. Her thumb sweeps across the glass, killing the alarm.

She looks back up at Ery, her spine straightening. "The gondola boards in twenty minutes," Jules murmurs, her voice steadying as she gently taps the soft fabric of Ery's sleeve. "Let's go get the others."

CHAPTER

Under the Stratosphere

The curved glass doors seal shut with a weighty thud, cutting off the chaotic clatter of the alpine crowds. Inside the suspended cabin, the enclosed air thickens with the heat of melting snow and damp wool. Frost grows at the edge of the panoramic windows, catching the condensation of exhausted breaths as the gondola pulls away from the earth.

The dimensions of the carriage halt Koa's momentum. The lack of floor space forces his grip to unclench, dropping massive stuffed shopping bags onto the grated metal. He slumps backwards into the curved plastic bench, wiping the dampness from his palms onto his knees.

As the gondola pierces the final veil of the lower cloud line, a blinding, sprawling expanse of the Swiss Alps floods the panoramic glass. Jules stares out into the infinite jagged white horizon. Her thumb, which had been tapping the rigid plastic edge of her itinerary for the past few hours, stops. Beside her, Minty's frame completely fills the remaining space within the cabin, leaning forward, her hooves shuffling on the steel grate. She presses her palms against the freezing glass, her wide eyes reflecting the azure sky above.

The groan of the deceleration wheel rings out before the doors hiss open at the Les Attelas overlook. The atmosphere thins out, razor sharp and painfully crisp, biting through exposed cheeks amidst the aggressive scent of high-altitude ozone. The powder of the peak stretches outward, glittering beneath the final minutes of the sun. Ery stays clinging firmly to Jules's side as their sneakers crunch through the frost, their thin soles providing a stark contrast to the thick thermal parkas they had layered over their clothes. Reaching a flat exposed crest of gravel, the group swings a heavy, woven wool picnic blanket against the breeze, the fabric catching the wind like a sail before settling flat across the ground.

They collapse into a heap, shedding the bulky thermal gear they had acquired in the village and piling the coats to one side of the blanket. Jules reaches into a shopping bag and produces a small, battery-operated lantern; as she twists the dial, it emits a low, pulsing warmth and a soft amber glow. Ery sinks her weight against Jules, her spine unspooling as her head rests against Jules's shoulder. Ery's amber eyes watch the slow, sweeping arc of Minty's tail against the snow.

"Do you think," Ery murmurs, her airy voice floating through the howl of the alpine air, "that if you hadn't crashed your skiff, we'd still be here? Or if I hadn't been standing in the rain that day, or if Minty hadn't written back?"

She extends her hand out to the cool air, watching snowflakes catch the wind and gently fly into the distance.

Koa swallows a mouthful of lukewarm pastry, leaning back on his palms. He looks across the warm glow of the lantern at the group. "If you didn't pull me out of the mud, you mean." He chuckles lightly, before looking down at his sneakers. "I'd still be dragging my feet around everywhere."

Minty shifts her hooves, leaning closer to the centre of the blanket, her tail loosely wrapping around her ankles. "I'm glad you all gave me a place to stay," she mumbles.

Jules looks down at Ery resting against her shoulder, her thumb brushing the soft fur of her hand. As the sun sinks behind the lip of the horizon, Jules watches the light across the valley below slowly bleed away. She turns back towards the group and breathes in deeply.

"I spent my entire life trying to architect a foundation that wouldn't collapse," she says, her voice lowering, her gaze tracking from Koa's wet laces to the curve of Minty's hooves. "I used to think, if I could plan for-"

CHAPTER

92

Viscous dampness clings to thick layers of processed hide, pressing a deep cold against pale skin. The air tastes of stale ozone. Sharp claws twitch, scraping blindly against an unseen, smooth surface. Blackness presses in from all sides, leaving eyes with nothing to latch onto. She shifts, her wings giving a small involuntary ripple to shed the weight of the atmosphere. Far ahead, a sharp pinprick of luminescence bleeds through the dark.

She drags her weight forwards, knuckles and fingertips pressing against a frigid floor. Her four limbs carry her forward towards the distant glow.

The concept of hours dissolves entirely,

Reduced to a repetitive scuff of roughened fabrics dragging across the ground,

The constant humming vibration deep in her chest,

The distant point of light dilates agonisingly slowly, expanding outward. As she breaches the threshold, pulling herself into the singularity of the glow, the sheer force of the light strips away the darkness, flooding her wide eyes with a broken expanse of burning white.

The brightness dissipates, dissolving into a still mist that coats her skin with a viscous dew. The air smells of damp greenery. Through the thick, grey air, a solitary silhouette stands amidst the expanse. The figure stands quietly atop a large square of dry, woven textile spread over the damp blades of grass. A faint, old scent of warm food drifts from the figure, a scent that causes her hands to twitch at her sides and her body to freeze.

She approaches in a slow sweep, breathing shallowly. Her claws tap against the fabric's border before dropping her weight onto the dry weave. Her fingertips knead the material playfully.

"The sun was warm by the water today," a soft voice murmurs beside her, the tone vibrating with a terrifying warmth. "I sat and watched the boats leave the harbour."

She flinches, her shoulders drawing sharply inward. A stinging pressure builds behind her eyes. Her throat tightens and she opens her mouth.

"I was waiting," she whispers, voice small, cracking in the damp air. "I waited so long."

The air chills, the ozone turning sharp. Without a sound, the slight, weighted depression in the fabric smooths itself flat. The faint smell evaporates completely into the suffocating tang of chemicals.

Her breath hitches. Her eyes snap to the right, her fingers frantically scraping across the thick textile. The fabric is perfectly level. She blinks, shaking her head, staring into the dead fog, her spine snapping back into rigid alignment.

She is alone. And that is safe.

And that is safe.

Safe.

Act 1

Chapters 1 - 6

CHAPTER

01

Bitter Mud

The crisp, alpine wind is gone.

Ery's amber eyes snap open. Her hand blindly grasps out, expecting to find the thick wool of the picnic blanket or the sleeve of Jules's jacket. Her fingers sink deep into freezing, viscous mud.

Her stomach violently contracts. She rolls to her side and vomits into the dark earth, staining it in pale fluid. Her chest heaves, but instead of the thin, clean air of the Alps, she pulls in ragged, wet gasps of stale ozone. The burn scrapes down her throat, leaving a harsh tang of copper on her tongue.

She forces her trembling knees into the slush. The pristine white snow of the overlook has been replaced by a sprawling stretch of damp dirt, softly bubbling with acidic decay. A dense, weeping fog swallows the landscape in every direction, casting a flat, shadowless light. Towering above dead flora loom colossal, decaying metal lattices. The iron giants spear upwards, their rusted peaks vanishing into the void, anchored to the earth by massive black power cables.

A heavy, rhythmic suction of boots tearing through the muck vibrates up her soles as she attempts to pull herself forwards.

Ery's antennae flick forward, catching a subtle displacement in the air. Her pulse hammers against her ribs. Frantic, she scrambles backwards, driving her weight into a dense thicket of abrasive brush. Jagged thorns rake across her cardigan, snagging deep in her neck fluff and scraping across her skin, but she locks her jaw shut. Dropping flush against the freezing mud, she drags her soaked wings over her head, shrinking her silhouette.

Through a fracture in the branches, she watches a solitary figure pierce the fog. The stranger moves with terrifying, mechanical precision, her weight distributed flawlessly across a compact, taur-like lower half. Four powerful, heavily booted limbs step through the sludge in calculated synchrony, anchored by the slow, stabilizing sweep of a thick tail behind her.

She pulls the caustic air into her lungs with an unbothered rhythm, her startlingly pale skin mapped with a violent tapestry of surgical scars and chemical burns. Draped awkwardly over her tactical gear is a faded, loose researcher's coat, the back heavily slit to accommodate the rugged wings folded tight against her spine. At the tips of the pinions, sharp, hooked claws glint in the flat light, twitching with the same rigid energy as her hands while the oversized hem of her coat drifts through the ozone.

The stranger halts abruptly. She kneels beside the dead power line, extending a bare hand to press her fingertips across the cool casing. Ery watches the muscles in the stranger's jaw lock tight. Her chest hitches in a sharp gasp. For a fraction of a second, her fingers twitch violently against the dead rubber. Then, just as quickly, her spine snaps rigid, her expression flattening.

The stranger rises in a single, fluid motion. Her head pivots. Purple and gold heterochromatic eyes cut a sharp, dead line straight towards the thicket.

Her arm snaps up, launching a sharp chunk of shale directly at the brush. The stone shatters the brittle thorns mere inches from Ery's face. Before the splintered wood even hits the ground, fingers plunge through the canopy, locking onto the heavy wool of Ery's cardigan.

Ery is violently hauled out the bush, her boots dragging through the muck. Her massive wings spasm outward in a frantic flutter, her pulse thrashing visibly at the base of her throat as she is forced to meet the demi-human's unblinking stare.

The grip tightens. The stranger tilts her head, analysing the twitch of Ery's antennae.

"Ery!"

A racking cough tears through the fog. Koa crashes through the brush, his chest heaving rapidly beneath his torn cardigan. His sneakers skid across the mire, sinking deep into the sludge. He throws his weight forward, but his knees buckle against the freezing mud as another coughing fit rattles his ribs.

A clatter of hooves strikes the dirt. Minty bursts into the

clearing. Her large hands grip the sides of her head, her eyes watering profusely against the stinging ozone. Spotting the scarred stranger suspending Ery, Minty lets out a choked gasp, immediately curling her spine forward to shrink her frame beneath the crushing scale of the iron towers above.

Jules breaks through a second later. Her cloudy glasses are entirely fogged over, her breathing a series of shallow wheezes.

She lunges. Her sneakers sink into the sludge as she plants herself squarely in the stranger's peripheral vision.

"Let her go!" Jules commands. The syllables crack halfway through, her voice thin. "What are you? Where did you take us?!"

The stranger does not flinch. Her grip remains locked on Ery's collar. The demi-human's eyes flick from Jules's shaking hands to the mucus Koa is coughing onto the mud, sweeping over their thin clothing and rapidly failing oxygen intake.

Slowly, her fingers unspool. Ery drops unceremoniously into the slush.

Ery's legs immediately give out. Koa scrambles through the mud, grabbing her sleeves to drag her upright, both of them hacking against the chemical burn in their throats.

Turning her back to the group entirely, the stranger resumes kneeling beside the dead power line. Her pupils dilate, darting across the worn rubber.

"The localised magnetic anchors have ceased," the stranger states. She traces the rubber with a fingertip, her tone a flat drone directed at the cable. "Your displacement is the causal factor. You have damaged my home."

Jules shakes her head, stepping backward to physically shield Ery and Koa. "That doesn't make sense. We were just in Switzerland. We're on a mountain." Jules rips her smartphone from her coat pocket. She taps the screen, but the glass remains dead black.

The stranger's head pivots. She looks at the dead piece of glass in Jules's hand, then back to the wheezing, hyperventilating humans.

"Your atmospheric intake is inefficient," the stranger drones. "The ambient ozone concentration is actively corrosive to your unshielded tissue. Your cellular degradation will accelerate. You are dying."

The words are clinical. Koa stares at the pale demi-human, his knuckles stark white where he grips Ery's sweater.

"Please," Koa begs, a wet wheeze rattling his ribs. He extends a shaking, mud-caked hand. "Please. Just tell us how to fix it."

The stranger recoils. Her weight shifts backward, her upper lip pulling taut over her teeth as if his outstretched hand carried a contagion.

"I am not a retrieval unit." Her eyes snap away from his face, sweeping upward to the decaying iron lattice vanishing into the grey void. A minute flutter disturbs her eyelids, her jaw locking tight. "However... your biological signatures possess bypass utility for the automated terminals at the peaks. If you provide authorization to restart the grid, I will direct auxiliary power to an evacuation threshold, and purge your mass from my sector."

She does not wait for a consensus.

Turning her back on the four of them, her coat sweeps over the dead power line as she steps directly into the mist. She doesn't look over her shoulder. She begins tracking a precise path, her silhouette dissolving into the miasma.

Jules's jaw tightens until the muscle twitches. She looks down at the dead phone in her hand. She looks at Ery, who is trembling so violently she can barely stand, and Minty, whose lungs are audibly straining against the viscous air. The math is agonizingly simple.

"Stay close," Jules breathes, her voice barely a whisper.

Jules drags her boots forward, leading her family blindly into the freezing unknown.

CHAPTER

Outworlders

For hours, the wet suction of shoes against the humid earth serves as their only metronome.

The caustic ozone strips the moisture from the outworlders' throats, leaving a sickly copper residue that forces Koa into chest-racking coughs. Minty's large frame sags under the suffocating pressure, her hooves sluggish through the marsh. Jules marches just behind their guide, wiping her glasses again after they fog up for the fourteenth time.

"Where are the nearest settlements? Why is it so hard to breathe? How far are we from the grid?" The syllables dissolve uselessly into the void. The demi-human does not turn. She maintains a pace the outworlders can barely keep, her wings occasionally twitching to shed the humid dew, deaf to the ragged breaths behind her.

Without warning, she halts at the precipice of a jagged fissure torn into the mud. The dead fog parts just enough to reveal a yawning, vertical drop lined with buckled steel. A stagnant downdraft bleeds up from the subterranean throat, coating the group's skin with the stench of oxidised iron and rotting, stale water. Through the dry dirt clinging to the reinforced bulkhead, a faded, geometric insignia remains faintly visible against the rusted metal.

The stranger pivots and steps into the sheer, collapsed chute. The descent is an oddly angled nightmare of warped steel. Her compact lower half absorbs the harsh incline, four boots distributing her weight across the treacherous surface. Extending straight back, her thick tail locks into a counterbalance that centres her mass. She displaces the stale air, the only acoustic disturbance the faint clicks of sharp claws at the tips of her wings hooking into the oxidised wall grates to stabilize her glide.

The outworlders plunge into the suffocating shaft, but the rusted pitch of the metal immediately rejects their presence. Minty's broad frame lacks the dexterity of their guide. Her hard hooves finding zero traction on the slick steel, she slips, her weight crashing sideways. A jarring, high-pitched screech of keratin against iron echoes up the chute. Behind her, Jules, Koa, and Ery stumble down the incline, their raw fingers scraping against the damp walls for any semblance of friction.

The descent terminates, dumping the outworlders into a pool of freezing, stagnant rainwater. The air is dead, sealed off from the caustic downdraft of the surface. Absolute blackness swallows the room, the heavy, reinforced walls of the subterranean bunker absorbing the echoing sounds of their hyperventilation.

The dim light from the outside bleeds just enough to reveal the knee-deep water before them.

A sharp crack splinters the dark.

The girl's pale fingers snap a polymer cylinder. A chemical reaction hisses within the tube, flooding the cramped chamber with a blue luminescence. The light carves the brutalist geometry of the room, casting towering, distorted shadows across the weeping concrete. Lined haphazardly across the flooded floor sit rows of massive, utilitarian supply containers, their sealed latches half-swallowed by the murky waters.

The blue light catches the glint of a polished, rectangular plate bolted to the concrete beside the heavy supply lockers. Jules leans forward, her sneakers sloshing through the knee-deep water as she swipes her thumb across the etched surface to clear a layer of oily silt. Beneath the grime lies a single line of text:

AXIOM HABITAT INITIATIVE
PROJECT FERMATA

Wading effortlessly through the freezing water, the stranger halts before one of the lockers bolted to the concrete wall. Her claws lock onto the hefty steel latch. With a sharp screech, she forces the mechanism upwards, breaking a centuries-old vacuum seal with a hiss. Inside, meticulously packed shelves hold the preserved remnants of survival.

Stacked rows of thick, insulated thermal suits sit beside breathing canisters and basic tools. Packed into the lower compartments are vacuum-sealed bags of dry rations and rows of metallic tubes, which leak a pungent, foul-smelling chemical odour of into the airless room.

Reaching into the dark compartment, she extracts one of the tubes. Her eyes snap to the faded text on the casing, pupils darting rapidly to process the data.

"Standard scientific expedition loadout," she drones, rotating the tube in her hand. Her gaze sweeps over the exhausted outworlders huddled in the freezing water. "Given your low biological mass, these resources will be a surplus for your expedition. Nobody will come for these in a long time."

The statement is followed by drained huffs and an oppressive quiet. The silence and the biting chill of the water gnaw at Koa. Forcing himself forward, his soaked sneakers splash through the flooded floor as he wedges himself beside the demi-human. He zeroes in on a canvas survival duffel jammed into the bottom rack. Locking his hands around the stiff handles, his chest heaves as he throws his entire body weight backward. His shoulders strain, but the impossibly dense bag refuses to yield from its lodged position.

The stranger's eyes cut towards him. She steps directly into his space, her shoulder driving him aside, and locks her pale hands onto the thick canvas straps. In a single motion, she rips the bag from the corroded floor, launching the sheer mass into the centre of the room. A spray of stagnant water crashes against the concrete walls. Koa stumbles backward, his jaw grinding. His eyes dart toward the floor as he tugs the damp sleeves of his cardigan over his palms.

Breaching the surface effortlessly, the stranger digs her clawed boots into the acidic slush and single-handedly hauls the final two survival duffels over the lip of the fissure. She drops the leaden canvas into the mud with a wet thud. Sitting in front of the group lie six duffel bags full of survival tools, rations and fresh water. She scans the void.

"Your life support. Your caloric expenditure. Carry it."

Koa's jaw tightens. He lunges forward, gathering the thick straps of three separate bags. The localised weight forces his spine to bow, the canvas straps digging into his collarbone, but he forces a strained grimace, his knuckles turning white to mask the tremor in his arms. Ery, Minty, and Jules each grab a single duffel from the mud. Minty's ears flicker nervously as she watches Koa's trembling knees, while Ery shrinks further into her neck fluff. Jules watches Koa's shuddering posture before pivoting to the other girls, marching up to Ery and Minty and yanking the slack from their canvas straps, snapping thick plastic buckles into place.

The march slowly grinds the outworlders down. Ery's breathing fractures into sharp gasps, her throat seizing tight as a pulse of heat radiates up her right ankle. She bites down on her bottom lip, her antennae pressing flat against her skull. Ducking her chin deep into the matted fur on her neck, she wraps her wings over the strap of her bag to cocoon her shivering torso. She begins to drag her right foot across the jagged earth, her gait falling behind the pace of their guide.

Jules sweeps the perimeter of the weeping fog, her neck pulled taut as she counts the silhouettes of her family. Her head snaps back, eyes locking onto the jarring, asymmetrical drag of Ery's right boot against the sludge. She closes the distance in three strides. Her hand shoots out, clamping onto Ery's shoulder to halt her momentum. Before Ery can stammer, Jules grabs the thick canvas strap and yanks it off her shoulder, dropping the dead weight into the mud with a splat. Locking onto Ery's shivering hands, Jules forces the moth-girl downward until her weight collapses onto the discarded duffel.

Dropping her full weight into the slush, Jules sinks deep into the mud. Her fingers tear at the thick laces of Ery's boot, peeling the wet leather away from her foot. She presses her thumbs firmly against the hot, inflamed flesh of the swollen ankle. Lifting her head, her voice cuts through the mist toward the retreating silhouette of their guide.

"Wait here for a little bit. We can't continue until the swelling stops."

Wait here.

Wait.

Here.

The demi-human's mechanical rhythm shatters. Her boots stop dead in the caustic muck.

Beneath the flat light of the void, her pupils dilate. A localised tremor rips up her spine, causing the clawed wings above the faded researcher's coat to tremble against the stitched fabric.

Spinning on her heels, the stranger's unbothered rhythm is instantly replaced by sharp, hyperventilating gasps tearing through the ozone. Her hand blurs downward, locking onto a tactical glaive strapped flush against her thigh holster.

The blade releases a high-pitched whistle as it's ripped free. She closes the distance in a single surge, rusted mud spraying from her boots as she levels the gleaming steel point directly at the centre of Ery's shivering chest. The muscles in her forearm lock tight, her entire taur frame shuddering beneath her oversized coat as her eyes bore through the terrified moth-girl.

"NOBODY IS COMING BACK FOR YOU!"

The scream tears raw through the suffocating fog. The sheer volume shatters her monotone drone, her vocal cords cracking. Her chest heaves as her upper lip pulls back into a desperate snarl, the blade trembling inches from Ery's collarbone. "Waiting… is how you die in the dark."

The outworlders are paralysed.

The thick canvas strap slips out of Koa's grip, his massive duffel crashing into the sludge with a heavy splash. Minty's frame jerks backward, her hooves scrambling against the dirt as she throws her hands tightly over her head. Jules throws her own body into the path of the gleaming steel. Wrapping both arms fiercely around Ery's trembling shoulders and pinning the moth-girl flush against her chest, Jules tilts her chin up. Her glasses reflect the trembling tip of the blade as she glares straight down the weapon's shaft.

The leaden steel of the glaive shakes, the tremor radiating up the pale, scarred arm. Her dilated pupils dart between the blade and Jules's torso. Hyperventilation hitches in her throat. She shakes her head quickly, her exposed teeth grinding together audibly.

Just as suddenly as it arrived, the trembling in her arm ceases. With a single, robotic motion, she rips the blade away from Jules's chest and slides it back into the holster. The mechanism seats the metal edge with a click.

The stranger turns. Her coat sweeps over the mud as she pivots her four boots back towards the endless white void, severing her visual connection to the outworlders.

Jules releases a fraction of the tension in her grip, her breathing shallow and rapid. She pulls the shivering girl closer, jaw tight, her unblinking gaze locked with defensive intensity onto the back of the retreating monster.

CHAPTER

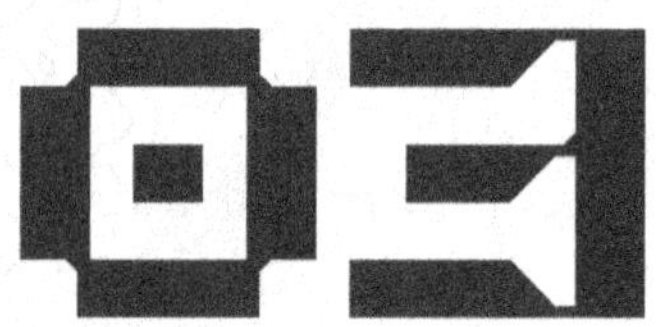

This Isn't Home

A sickening, low-frequency tectonic grind vibrates up out of the acidic slush, rattling the teeth in their skulls. The viscous atmosphere presses against their chests, forcing every shallow, ragged breath to drag a tang of copper down their throats. The terrain is a jagged nightmare of calcified, rotting roots that twist out the earth like shattered bones.

The stranger halts her pace, her four boots planting firmly into the uneven earth. She adjusts the collar of her coat as physical exhaustion forces the outworlders to collapse. Koa's shoulders sag beneath his cardigan, his chest heaving with rattling coughs as he drops his three canvas duffels into the muck. Beside him, Ery drags her right boot with a mild limp, the hem of her mud-drenched skirt catching on the jagged roots as she sinks against a calcified trunk.

Koa, Ery, and Minty take the time to dig into the heavy survival bags, pulling out the thick thermal coats to seal their bodies against the biting damp, while Jules remains in her utilitarian coat.

Jules steps away from the group. Her sight snaps towards the sprawling, unpredictable tangle of calcified roots. The complete absence of straight lines and predictable geometry keeps her breath trapped in her throat. Dropping her canvas bag onto the ground, she immediately begins carving strict, intersecting tracks through the sludge with her sneakers.

As Jules attempts to anchor thick nylon fabrics, the metal pegs slide through the damp dirt. The shallow, fibrous grass and loose soil reject her designated structure. It quickly gives way under the tension, causing the pegs to slip free and the thick canvas to sag into an uneven, slumped pile.

Jules's knuckles turn white. She drops her full weight to her knees, gripping the metal stakes to force them deeper into the wet earth.

She slams the mallet down, her jaw locked so tight her teeth ache. On a desperate downward strike, the stake hits a subterranean shelf of calcified stone and skids sideways. Jules's momentum carries her entire weight forward; her palm slides off the rain-slicked metal and slams directly onto a jagged, upright root protruding from the muck like a serrated tooth. The calcified tip tears through the nylon mesh of her glove and anchors deep into the meat of her palm. Her head snaps back, a sharp, choked gasp dying in her throat as her heart thrashes. She winces, her teeth bared in a silent snarl as she yanks her hand free from the root with a tear.

Muddy sneakers splash heavily into the wet grass right beside Jules's hunched shoulders.

A dark, thin trail of blood begins to seep into the sludge from beneath her hand, the copper scent rising to meet the ozone. Koa's chest rattles with another cough, his sleeves pulled down as he bears a strained smile. He reaches for the collapsed canvas, his hands grabbing at the misaligned stakes. He pauses, his eyes widening as he tracks the crimson smear spreading across the root and the nylon.

"Here, let me get that side," he pants, wrestling the tent pole into place. His shoulder bumps hard against Jules, knocking her off balance.

She claps the injury against her chest, fresh blood pulsing between her fingers and staining the front of her cargo jacket. Her free hand pushes her glasses back up into place. "Koa, stop. You're throwing off the tension on the guidelines."

"I've got it. It's just-" Koa pulls harder, sending the canvas sideways.

"Koa." Jules's voice sharpens, cutting through the damp air. She rips the canvas strap out of his grip with her good hand, her arm tucked tightly against her ribs.

"Go sit down. You are in the way."

Koa's smile falters. He looks down at his empty hands, then retreats to the edge of the grove.

The stranger tracks the exchange with cold eyes, tracking Jules's shallow breathing and the highly visible grid she is carving into the dead earth. Moving up to her, she sends one of the pegs flying out of the dirt with a swift kick.

Jules shoots up from the mud.

Her hands weakly curl into fists at her sides, her chest heaving as she glares directly at the demi-human.

A pale finger extends, pointing directly at the lines Jules had carved into the sludge. "Symmetry does not exist in this biome," she drones. "Rigid geometric lines project a high-visibility, unnatural contrast against irregular organic structures. You are constructing a beacon for anyone who wants to kill us." She turns, pacing back to the perimeter of the camp.

Just a moment later, Minty's hard hooves scrape against the damp dirt as she attempts to compress her large body into the irregular, shadowed alcove. Her long tail tucks between her hind legs.

"Sorry, sorry..." she mutters under her breath, her voice trembling as she tries to drag her heavy canvas bag closer to her chest. "I can move further out."

Squeezing her eyes shut, Jules digs her fingers tightly into the bridge of her nose. Her chest heaves with a long exhale that catches in her throat.

"Minty, just stop moving," Jules snaps, her voice cracking with exhaustion. "Just sit down, please."

Minty's shoulders draw sharply inward, and she sinks into the damp grass in silence.

The outworlders huddle miserably around the smokeless heat of a chemical fire, their thick coats pulled flush against the chill to share their first rationed dinner. Sleep deprivation drags at their eyelids.

Deep beneath the shallow grass, a low-frequency tectonic

grind continuously vibrates up through the soles of their shoes.

Koa sits at the edge of the pale light, his jaw tight. He yanks the wet laces of his sneakers, tying them into complex knots, only to pull them loose and start over.

Across the dim fire, Ery clutches a foiled sachet of dense, synthetic soup. Her feathery antennae droop against her forehead, her teardrop wings wrapped tightly around her shivering shoulders. She stares blankly at the pale orange ration, her mouth pressed into a thin line.

Koa's hands pause on his laces. He extends his own half-eaten, mildly flavoured fibrous block towards her. "Here. You need to eat."

Ery slowly shakes her head, shrinking further into her thick neck fluff.

Beside them, Jules does not look up from her lap. She methodically bites off a piece of the dense ration with one hand, chewing the dry substance without a change in expression. Her right hand, wrapped in a makeshift, blood-bloated bandage of grey gauze, is wracked with tremors as she attempts to carve jagged lines of notes across a fresh notebook. The pen slips repeatedly against the paper, the ink smearing into illegible, dark stains.

Removed from the tight, shivering circle of the outworlders, the stranger stands at the perimeter of the pale firelight. Her back is turned towards the camp, her four legs folded underneath her in the cold dirt. She is perfectly still. Not a single muscle twitches in her compact frame.

Only her eyes move, darting across the mist to pierce the pitch-black fog, scanning the dead grove like a living mechanical alarm.

Minty pushes herself up, her hooves thumping softly against the roots. She halts a few paces behind the demi-human, immediately curving her spine and pulling her shoulders down.

"You could use one of the canvas tents," she whispers, her voice trembling slightly. "To rest. There's enough room for everyone."

The thump of hooves against dirt breaks the stranger's stillness. The hooked claws at the tips of her wings twitch. Beneath the shadow of her collar, her pupils dilate.

"Enclosed spaces eliminate critical escape vectors," she drones, her voice flattening to a razor-thin line of data. She doesn't turn to acknowledge the taur, her unblinking gaze locked entirely on the black void.

Minty's hands tighten against the fraying fabric of her winter coat. Her fingers dig deep into the lining of her pocket. They emerge clutching a small cluster of bulbous, berry-like indigenous flora she had scavenged from the edge of the grove hours prior.

Her hand trembles slightly as she steps closer, extending her open palm into the demi-human's peripheral vision. "Here, you didn't eat any of the rations."

The stranger freezes.

She recoils. Her frame jerks sharply backwards, her hooves scrambling against the freezing mud. Her arm snaps upward with blinding speed.

A sharp snap echoes through the dead grove.

The stranger strikes Minty's hand with enough force to send the fruit flying out of her palm. It hits the damp dirt with a wet thud, and before it can settle, her heavy boot instantly crushes the scavenged flora deep into the toxic slush.

Minty gasps, her hooves stumbling backwards as she quickly pulls her stinging hand to her chest.

The stranger's upper lip peels over her teeth. Her chest heaves with hyperventilating gasps, her eyes wide as she glares at the trembling taur. The muscle in her jaw twitches as she wrestles her breathing back down to baseline.

"You are defective," she states, her voice dropping to her monotone drone. Her fingers release from white-knuckled fists at her sides. "First, disrupting camp operations, and second, allocating caloric resources to a non-essential variable. You are mathematically suicidal."

Around the chemical fire, the tying of laces stops. The scratching of a metal pen ceases. Jules, Koa, and Ery stare out into the freezing perimeter, watching the taur shrink before the scarred demi-human.

CHAPTER

Where Lost Things Die

Sheer, brutalist concrete walls rise on either side, their tops swallowed by the weeping fog, funnelling the caustic ozone into a corridor. Thick, oxidised rebar curls from the fractured ferrocrete. A slick, iridescent layer of toxic runoff coats the ground, pooling deep inside jagged fissures. The atmospheric pressure presses down on the group, compounding the harsh, echoing drip of acidic condensation falling from the canopy to slap against hard stone.

Koa hauls his three survival duffels, the canvas straps digging deep into the shoulders of his thermal coat. His sneaker hydroplanes across a patch of runoff, sliding across the slime until the tip catches against an oxidised iron grate. His joint buckles. He forces his mouth shut, tugging his sleeves over his palms to hide the tremor in his hands, hitching the bags higher up his shoulder despite the asymmetrical drag of his right foot.

It's not long before the stranger's eyes lock onto the uneven scrape of Koa's sneaker against the wet stone. Her gaze tracks his sagging foot. Beneath the faded collar of her coat, her pupils shift, calculating the acoustic drag and the asymmetrical deficit in his stride.

She pivots. Her four boots plant directly onto a slab of cracked concrete, barricading his path. Koa halts, his chest heaving under the suffocating atmospheric pressure as he looks up at the demi-human.

"Your compromised mobility is reducing our transit efficiency." She takes in a breath, her flat tone echoing off the high spillway walls. "Offload your excess cargo."

Stepping directly into his personal space, her pale hands reach out and lock onto the thick canvas strap of his heaviest duffel. She shifts her stance towards a jagged fissure brimming with toxic runoff, preparing to heave the excess mass.

Koa jerks his shoulder backwards. He wraps both arms around the bag, digging his fingers into the heavy canvas. A bitter tug-of-war ensues over the slick stone. The muscles beneath the stranger's scarred skin pull. Yet, Koa throws his entire failing body weight in the opposite direction. His wet sneakers slide helplessly across the wet stone, roughly grinding as he growls against the pull. A deep flush crawls up his neck to his cheeks, his eyes wide and watering as he fights against her grip.

The demi-human stalls. Her head tilts as she stares down at Koa's straining, sweating face.

Desperate for leverage Koa slides his injured foot back, planting the heel of his sneaker against a jutting stalk of oxidised rebar. He yanks the canvas. The compromised ankle joint buckles completely under the sheer tension. His grip fails. He collapses, crashing hard, face-first against the ferrocrete.

The stranger rips the canvas bag upwards. Under the sudden, sheer force, the rusted metal buckle snaps with a sharp crack. The thick canvas splits open.

A clatter of metal and synthetic polymer casing rings out against the high spillway walls as the leaden survival tools and dense rations spill across the stone. Among the steel frames and blackened iron, a cracked, silver analogue watch and a small, laminated family photograph slide across the ground, coming to rest in a shallow puddle of condensation.

A patter begins to strike the concrete. Cold, clean rain pierces the fog, washing over the toxic runoff.

The demi-human halts her motion. She drops to a kneel on the cold stone. Her pale fingertips pinch the edge of the laminated photograph, pulling it free from the shallow puddle. Her eyes track across the glossy surface. She winces, rotating it slowly beneath the rain.

Koa's raw fingers dig into the slick ferrocrete, his knees sliding as he scrambles. With terrified speed, his hand blurs forward and snatches the photograph directly out of the monster's pale grip. He throws his weight backwards, clutching it tightly against his heaving chest, hacking a wet cough into the collar of his coat to protect it from the downpour.

Jules stands rigid a few paces down the spillway, behind a shivering Minty and Ery. Her cloudy glasses are streaked with fresh rain. her gaze locks onto the demi-human. As Koa pulls the photograph away, the stranger's mechanical stare completely drops. For a second, a minute flutter of longing passes through her heterochromatic eyes as she watches Koa desperately shelter the paper.

Then, her spine snaps straight.

Her eyes sweep over the broken canvas straps, the shattered rations, and the cracked analogue watch half-submerged in the runoff.

She pivots, her hefty boots striking the wet stone as she pronounces her departure, clicks echoing down the suffocating corridor as she walks away into the fog.

Koa's hands shake violently. He drops the photograph into his coat pocket and lunges forward, his raw fingers desperately clawing at the ripped canvas. He attempts to force the snapped metal buckle back together, his breath catching in ragged gasps as he shoves heavy iron tools back into the ruined bag.

A hand presses firmly against his shoulder.

Jules kneels beside him on the cold stone. A sharp, hot pulse of pain radiates from the bandaged tear in her palm as she leans her weight against the stone to steady herself. The rain streaks her glasses as she looks down at his bleeding knuckles and the gigantic tear in the fabric.

"Koa," she says quietly, her voice soft and low. She tightens her grip on his shoulder. "Leave it."

Night falls, bleeding the white fog into a bruised charcoal. The outworlders drag their exhausted, shivering bodies up a sheer, oxidised utility stairwell at the end of the spillway. The climb terminates on the massive, sweeping curve of a decayed dam.

A sheer drop plunges into the pitch-black fog on one side, while the other is bordered by a monolithic corroded retaining wall. The sharp drip of condensation striking the cracked stone amplifies the immense emptiness of the structure.

Pinned against the base of the retaining wall, the group presses their shoulders together to hoard the anaemic warmth of a chemical ignition cube. They sit with their knees drawn tightly to their chests, the thick collars of their thermal gear zipped flush to their jawlines to block out the damp, biting crosswind sweeping over the edge of the dam. Distorted shadows cast by the harsh light stretch up the brutalist concrete, shrinking the family into tiny, isolated silhouettes perched atop a dead world.

Jules presses her spine against the cold stone wall. The throbbing in her palm has settled into a dull, rhythmic heat, making her fingers twitch as she shakily grips her metal pen, pointing the silver tip at the shivering boy to her left.

"Koa," Jules states into the dead air.

The pen shifts towards the taur. "Minty."

It sweeps towards the moth cocooned in her wings. "Ery. And I am Jules." She lowers the pen, letting the syllables hang over the gentle hiss of the chemical heat and the mild showering rain rolling down their coat hoods. "We should operate using these designations. It establishes a functional baseline for our communication."

She shifts her gaze to the perimeter of the light, staring directly at the solitary guide sitting motionless in the shadows.

"What is your name?"

The stranger stares at the reflection of the light in the wet concrete.

"92."

Minty's ears droop, pressing flat against the damp collar of her coat. She watches the scarred demi-human sitting across the fire.

"Do you have a real name?" she whispers.

The stranger's head tilts an inch. Her eyes slow to a halt. "I was assigned 92," she continues, her tone perfectly flat.

The silence stretches. The stranger's unblinking stare remains fixed on Minty, then to the flickering light of the ignition against the glistening ground. She sucks in air through her teeth.

She swallows, and struggles on the thin air, as if her lungs had suddenly flooded with thick fluid.

She lifts herself off the ground, stumbling backwards slightly, one of her boots catching awkwardly against the ferrocrete.

"Names are… inefficient emotional tethers." Her voice splinters. "Inquire about a non-essential designation again, and I will abandon your mass."

The outworlders are left staring into the geometric

shadows of the retaining wall.

Jules looks from the spot where the terrifying, hyper-lethal demi-human had just choked on thin air, down to the shivering, exhausted faces of her family. Jules grips her knees as she pulls herself closer to the meagre heat of the flame, preparing for a long, sleepless watch in the dark.

CHAPTER

A Lack of Awareness

Massive, hollowed-out cooling towers loom within the fog, their crumbling concrete choked by pale vines and curtains of translucent moss. The biting crosswind dies here, replaced by a stale atmosphere. Every laboured breath pulls the thick stench of rotting vegetation and caustic ozone deep into their lungs, compounding the physical weight of their soaked coats. Koa shifts his weight, the straps of his two remaining survival duffels digging into his bruised shoulders.

A raised steel grating offers a brief reprieve from the murky waters beneath, but Jules uses the time to pace tight, intersecting tracks across the platform, her chest rising and falling in shallow hitches. Pressing her metal pen against the back of her notebook, the silver tip bites so hard it tears through the paper. She crosses out jagged lines of desperate math, carving new numbers into the margins as she calculates the depreciation of their resources against their sluggish transit speed.

Perched on a deteriorating, rusted exhaust pipe removed from the group, the stranger watches the erratic pacing, tracking the scratching of the metal pen and the rapid rise and fall of Jules's chest.

The heavy silence of the swamp is paused only by Koa's racking coughs and the relentless tear of Jules's pen against paper. Minty clutches the fraying edges of her coat, her knuckles whitening. She steps forwards, her hooves clacking awkwardly against the steel grating. She softly reaches her hand out towards the pacing woman.

"Jules," Minty whispers over the stagnant air. "Please. The math won't change right now. We might need to sit down for a minute. Koa can't breathe."

Jules whips around, her hand aggressively shoving her glasses up the bridge of her nose. Her chest heaves with a ragged, shallow hitch.

"We are resting," Jules states, sharply and clipped against the ozone. "In fact, we have been resting for four minutes and eighteen seconds. Every minute we are not moving, we are poisoning our cells."

"But he's coughing up fluid," Minty pleads, her voice trembling, pointing a shaking hand back towards Koa slumped against the grating. "If we just let him catch his breath-"

"I am CALCULATING his breath!" Jules snaps, the raw volume tearing her voice. She lunges forwards, pointing the metal tip of her metal pen directly at the centre of Minty's chest. The notebook trembles violently in her hands.

"I don't even know what our caloric baseline is, but I know you need more than we do. Your stride is compromised by the terrain. Your hooves slip on majority of the surfaces we cross." Jules delivers the critique with hyper-vigilant speed. "I am trying to figure out how long we have before your inefficiencies drag our survival probability into the red."

Minty's ears instantly pin against her skull, absorbing her calculation. A sudden, cold wave of nausea washes over her features, her eyes watering.

Her jaw trembles. She pulls her coat tighter around her torso and backs away, hooves scraping quietly against the rusted steel as she retreats entirely from the group, disappearing into the dense, pale brush bordering the turbine.

Jules's hand drops.

The silence of the dead grove rushes in to replace her panicked volume, and her shoulders slump beneath her coat. She stares at the empty space on the grating. She reaches out a shaking hand towards the brush. "Minty," Jules whispers, the command sapped out of her voice. But the taur has already been swallowed by the fog.

Jules turns her head. Through a gap in the rusting machinery, her cloudy glasses catch sight of Ery. The moth-girl sits silently on the edge of an adjacent metal platform, her massive wings wrapped tightly around her waist, her amber eyes wide and fixed on Jules with a quiet concern that makes Jules instantly turn away.

Deep within the thick fog, Minty wades blindly through a pool of shallow runoff. Her hard hooves slip against submerged chunks of concrete, but she forces her frame forward into the industrial graveyard.

Through the dense, translucent moss hanging from the structures, a faint shape catches her eye. Clinging to the side of a fractured, submerged exhaust pipe grows a cluster of pale, bulbous flora, their smooth surfaces glistening with condensation. Minty's breath hitches. She reaches her hands out over the water, fingers trembling as she stretches to harvest the bulbs.

A thick tangle of oxidised rebar bites into Minty's trailing hoof. Her body pitches forward into the runoff. Her arms flail blindly against the stone, her right elbow crashing violently against the submerged exhaust pipe directly beside the pale flora.

The bulbs rupture.

A sharp, loud hiss cuts through the air. The disturbed flora vomits a dense, pressurized cloud of sickly yellow spores straight upward, corrosive dust expanding rapidly towards her face.

A hefty, desperate splash of wet sneakers tearing through the runoff shatters the hiss. Koa dives headfirst through the brush, his chest heaving as he slams his shoulder directly into Minty's waist. The momentum physically shoves the taur backwards, knocking her frame completely clear of the spore cloud. Koa hits the oxidised steel grating hard. His tattered jacket tears against the pipe as he skids to a halt beside Minty.

Koa groans, his shoulder pressed against the wet steel grating. He pushes himself up onto one knee, a louder cough tearing through his chest as he looks over his shoulder to check Minty scrambling backwards on the platform.

"I've... got... you..." Koa pants, his chest heaving.

He reaches his right arm across his body to wipe the condensation from his face.

The fabric of his thermal coat is completely torn from elbow to wrist. A jagged, bleeding scrape runs the length of his exposed forearm, carved by the rusted exhaust pipe. Surrounding the laceration, the pale skin is already swelling into a sickening, yellow rash where the spores had breached his bloodstream. His smile collapses, his eyes widening at the aggressive necrosis.

The stranger clears the distance in three massive bounds, her four hefty boots slamming down against the steel grating, planting a barricade between Minty and Koa.

Her heterochromatic pupils dilate, calculating the rate of the yellow burn accelerating across the compromised unit's tissue. Her pale arm snaps out straight, physically blocking Minty from lunging back towards the boy.

"Necrotic particulate is transmissible. Quarantine of contaminated unit," she drones, listing protocol. Her unblinking gaze locks on the caustic dust. "Physical contact guarantees secondary transfer. Application of textiles to a breached bloodstream is a critical waste of resources."

She holds her arm rigid against Minty's chest while her other hand reaches into the soot-stained lining of her coat. She pulls out a small silver, industrial cylinder tipped with a heavy-gauge needle. Inside the glass chamber, a sickly brown fluid sways with the motion. Pulling off a thin cap and thumbing the plunger to clear a bead of liquid at the tip, she levels the point toward the soft tissue of Koa's throat, her intent as clinical as a slaughterhouse bolt.

The skittish, conflict-averse taur lunges forward, throwing

her entire weight against the stranger's barricading arm. The violent, uncalculated shove physically knocks the hyper-lethal guide off balance. Her boots scrape against the grating.

The stranger is stunned into silence, watching Minty willingly cross the contamination line.

Dropping to her knees in the runoff, Minty grabs Koa's blistering arm, disregarding the sting transferring to her own bare palms. She frantically uses the frayed hem of her own coat to wipe the yellow particulate from his skin.

"I've got it, I've got it," Minty gasps, tears streaming down her face. "I'm sorry. I'm so sorry. Oh my god..."

Jules bursts through the brush a second later. Ignoring the demi-human entirely, she rips a satchel of filtered drinking water from her coat pocket. She unseals it, pouring the hydration directly over Koa's open, bleeding scrape before tightly binding the flesh in a roll of clean, medical gauze.

The stranger stares at the puddle of wasted drinking water seeping into the runoff. Her jaw locks tight.

Against the grate, Koa's chest heaves. He glances at Minty's burning hands, and Jules tightening the gauze around his arm. He wrenches his bound arm out of Minty's grip, pushing himself backwards against the rusted turbine.

"Stop looking at me like I'm a dying dog!" he roars. The volume strips his throat raw, sending him into a wet, agonizing coughing fit. He glares at the glistening grating, pulling his good sleeve tightly over his shaking hand. "I did my job! I'm fine! Just stop talking about it!"

Minty's hooves slip against the grating,

her knees buckling as she sinks back into the shallow

water, weeping quietly into her blistered hands. Koa stares at her shaking shoulders, his jaw grinding. He tumbles onto his undamaged side, unable to swallow the lump in his throat as he stares at a bead of condensation sitting on the grate.

Minty watches the stranger as she maintains the perimeter in absolute, statuesque silence, perched atop the high point of a nearby cooling tower. Her silhouette vanishes into the fog, save for the faint, steady darting of her eyes.

Minty looks toward the others. They take separate seats on the cold metal grating, heads resting against corroded pipes. Between them sits a scavenged lamp, buzzing with a harsh white fluorescent glare. The fifth bag, now entirely depleted of medical supplies and water after the treatment of Koa's wound, lies flat and useless against a rusted pipe in the dark.

Jules presses the back of her metal pen against her lips, her glasses glinting in the light. "We just use her tracking to reach the peaks," she whispers, keeping her voice low against the hum of the bulb. "The second the grid stabilises and we can get home, we cut her loose. We don't owe her anything else. It is a transaction."

Koa shifts his uninjured shoulder, his gaze dropping to the grating. "She doesn't need all of us to make it," he mutters, his throat rattling with a wet cough. "She said our biological signatures possess bypass utility. Just the signatures. If one of us slows her down, she cuts the weight. She's just waiting for the first of us to drop."

Jules lowers her pen. She looks at Koa's heavily bandaged arm, then across the grating at Ery's shivering form.

"She's doing it on purpose," Jules states, the syllables thin and sharp. "Look at how we are acting. She strips every action down to caloric cost and survival probability, and she forces us to do the same. She treats us like broken variables so we start treating each other the same way. She wants us to fracture. She is trying to turn us against each other so it's easier to leave someone behind."

At the edge of the dim light, Minty lowers her slowly recovering, stinging hands from her face. She stops wiping the tears from her cheeks. She lifts her chin, her gaze tracking slowly up the crumbling concrete of the tower to the solitary, unseen perch of the hyper-lethal guide waiting in the dark.

Minty slowly shakes her head. "No," Minty whispers, the soft syllables hanging heavy over the buzzing lamp.

Jules and Koa pause, turning their heads to look at the taur.

"She isn't mean because she hates us, or because she wants us to fail," Minty continues, her eyes dropping back to the harsh fluorescent bulb. "She's mean because she is terrified of us."

The stark light flickers against Jules's glasses and the hard line of Koa's jaw. Slowly, their gaze drifts upward, staring back into the pitch-black fog where the scarred, weaponized monster waits.

CHAPTER

Out of Sight

A thick layer of dried, chalky chemical sediment blankets the steep incline. Towering concrete battle blocks jut from the crust of the earth, forcing a narrow path through a claustrophobic maze of oxidised iron sluice gates. Fog settles, choking the spaces between the endless rows of identical, monolithic pillars, cutting visibility down to a few feet. Every footfall crunches against the sediment, kicking fine chalky dust into the caustic ozone.

Koa drags his sneakers through the dust. He hitches his two remaining survival duffels higher on his good shoulder, his frame bowing under the weight. Minty stays a marginal number of paces behind him, looking down at the pale dirt. Ahead of them both, the stranger marches, silent, unyielding.

Marching at the rear, Jules sweeps her sight over the line, counting the pale silhouettes cutting through the blinding mist.

Koa. Minty.

"Ery," Jules calls out into the mist, her voice thin.

Jules freezes. Her boots stop dead in the chalk.

The syllables hit the towering, identical concrete baffle blocks and instantly shatter. The sound bounces violently in every direction, the acoustic profile of the labyrinth fracturing her voice across the landscape. There is no response. The empty space behind Jules is swallowed by fog and settling white dust. Ery is gone.

Why do you keep...

Jules unclips her canvas duffel, dropping the weight into the chalky sediment with a muted thud. Pushing her glasses up to her nose, she points her metal pen into the blinding mist, heaving rapidly.

"We have to stop here," she demands, her voice cracking. She slashes her pen in a rigid square towards Koa and Minty. "Minty, you take the left flank. Koa, the right. I'm moving back through the centre. We grid-search outward from this exact location in ten-metre increments. Do not deviate. Do not step out of visual range of the next pillar."

The stranger halts, grinding to a stop against the chemical sediment. Her pupils dart rapidly through the mist,

her internal processing filtering the atmospheric density of the caustic ozone.

She pivots.

"Search operations expend critical caloric reserves and guarantee fatal degradation within this environmental density," she speaks cleanly over Jules's math. She doesn't blink. "Your unit, 'Ery', is a lost variable."

One more look over them settles her decision on the matter. The stranger's faded researcher's coat sweeps over the chalky sediment as she turns her back on the outworlders.

Koa scrambles across the loose shale, throwing his body between two rusted gates directly in the demi-human's path. Minty and Jules surge forward beside him physically barricading the route.

"You can't just leave her!" Koa screams, his voice tearing raw. "We aren't leaving without her!"

"She's out there, she's lost!" Jules yells. "You cannot make us leave this spot! We have the supplies, we have the gear, we are finding her!"

"Please!" Minty cries out, her voice breaking. "Please, just help us find her, you can't leave her alone!"

The sheer hostility physically strikes the demi-human, her boots scraping awkwardly backwards against the sediment. She stands still, staring at the three flushed, failing biological units barricading her path.

Rather than forcing passage, her boots lock onto the rough edge of a jagged concrete block just outside their defensive perimeter. She vaults atop the monolithic pillar in a single, fluid motion.

From her elevated perch, she pulls a mechanical chronometer from one of her hide pockets.

Her pale thumb depresses the brass button. The metallic click of the timer rings out, starting the count.

Her eyes immediately lock onto the frantic outworlders, her unblinking stare attempting to burn into their skulls.

Koa turns from the monster on the pillar to Jules and Minty. "We have to stay together," he pants, his chest racking another cough. He extends his unbandaged arm to Jules, whose grip clamps down on his palm. Minty's fingers wrap tight around Jules's opposite wrist, tethering the group together. They wade blindly back down into the biting mist.

Tick.

Tick.

Tick.

The outworlders drag their boots across the dry chemical sediment, their human chain weaving between the monolithic concrete teeth of the labyrinth. Jules produces a high-lumen flashlight from her scavenged duffel, its harsh beam pierces only a few feet before the airborne chalk reflects it back. The identical, rusted iron sluice gates distort their screams and yells for Ery, throwing the panicked noises back at them until their throats are raw and bleeding.

High atop the jagged concrete block, the brass hands of the chronometer click forward.

The stranger's eyes do not break contact with the small line of failing biological units below.

She internally logs their physical collapse. Koa spits out a thick stream of dark fluid into the shale. Minty stumbles, her frame shivering violently beneath her thermal coat as she struggles to drag her hooves through the dust. Jules is left with her shoulders caving inward as the viscous ozone and severe calorie deficit tear through her determination.

Yet, as the fog actively poisons their cells, as they grow sicker with every step, and as they starve, their grip on each other does not slip.

They will not abandon her.

The outworlders would rather physically expire in the chalk dust before severing their emotional tether. A tremor rips up the stranger's spine. The immediate prospect of the units freezing to death in the labyrinth slams into her processing. Within hours, she will be left entirely alone in the immense, dead silence again. Her jaw grinds together with a harsh, audible *clack*. She snaps the brass casing of the chronometer shut.

Dropping from the jagged baffle block, her four boots slam against the chemical sediment. Her faded coat sweeps aggressively past the shivering human chain. She does not look back at any of the outworlders, plunging straight into the blinding, pitch-black fog.

She tilts her head a fraction of an inch, eyes wincing. Her sensory processing overrides the dense, caustic ozone and the metallic tang of the rusted gates, until it isolates a faint trace of almond milk trapped in the white dust. She rips through the maze with apex speed. Her boots navigate the identical, acoustic dead-ends and towering concrete pillars with flawless precision, her trajectory unbothered by the zero-visibility miasma.

Minutes later, her silhouette breaches the fog line. Ery is huddled tightly against the base of a collapsed iron bulkhead, her massive teardrop wings pinned flat over her shivering thermal coat. Pale, small hands plunge through the mist, the stranger's fingers locking onto the collar of Ery's coat.

"Wh-" Ery gasps, her eyes snapping wide in sheer panic.

The stranger digs her boots into the chalky sediment and violently yanks Ery's collar, dragging the startled moth backward through the abrasive dust. The crunch of heavy boots fractures the silence surrounding the human chain. Jules, Koa and Minty whip their heads towards the sound.

The stranger breaches the fog line, hauling the dead weight of Ery behind her, before violently heaving her body forward so forcefully that it causes the faded, oversized researcher's coat to slip askew down the stranger's pale shoulder.

Ery is thrown face-first into the freezing chemical sediment directly at Jules's feet. A sharp gasp releases from Ery's lungs as she impacts the abrasive dust. She messily scrambles upward onto her forearms, her right arm collapsing under her pressure. She clutches her shoulder blade tightly, wincing.

Pushing herself out of the chalk, her eyes lock onto the exhausted, sickly faces of her family looking down at her in the dim light of the flashlight.

The sight of Koa's bloodshot eyes and Jules's collapsed, shivering posture breaks her.

Ery curls her spine inward, collapsing back into the dust. She throws her mud-stained wings tightly over her head. She buries her face deep into her neck fluff, cocooning her shivering frame to muffle a wet, messy sob.

The stranger's chest heaves aggressively beneath her coat. Her breathing shatters and jumps against the ozone, her eyes narrowing into a raw glare at the shivering human chain.

"You are statistically suicidal," she dictates, barely low through her gritted teeth. Her upper lip pulls taut over her mouth as she points a finger down at the weeping moth. "Allocating caloric reserves to a non-essential is a fatal processing error."

The outworlders stare at the furious, scarred monster in horrified silence.

Jules looks towards Koa and Minty, before turning back towards the unfeeling survival machine who had just burned her precious caloric reserved to retrieve the broken variable she was describing. The stranger draws an uncomfortably long breath in through her nose, before stomping forward into the dust.

Minty's eyes drop from the demi-human's glare to a small, white rectangular tag stitched into the old fabric. The title *Dr.* is printed in sharp, faded block letters, followed immediately by a thick scribble of black ink crossing out the original surname.

Neatly penned in soft, cursive script just beneath the redaction, is a single word:

Cadence.

Minty turns around to watch her friend shrivelled up in the dust.

Act 2

Chapters 7 - 11

CHAPTER

Lies That We Tell People

The wind howls.

It clears the stagnant ozone, surging across endless, rolling fields of ankle-high, deep crimson grass. Above, a translucent, shifting blanket of clouds stretches from horizon to horizon.

This sunlight rolls over the landscape in blinding waves, sweeping across the crimson fields in rhythmic pulses as the clouds fracture and reform. Harsh light strikes the rock formations in brief, intense bursts before plunging them back into bruised shadows. Without a canopy or cover, the skeletal powerlines march into the extreme distance to break the vast, churning horizon.

The outworlders squint at the brightness. Despite the raw

sunlight, the sweeping wind strips the heat straight from their skin. Jules pulls the collar of her coat flush against her jaw, her teeth clicking as the altitude temperature bites through the fabric.

At the edge of Jules's peripheral vision, their guide abruptly stalls. The stranger drops to her knees in the deep, rolling crimson grass. Her pupils dilate wildly against the bright azure sky. She stares blankly at the rippling horizon, her pale hands sinking into the vibrant soil. Her fingers gently comb through the blades, the stiff, unblinking sheet of ice melting from her as she kneads the soil.

The outworlders collapse onto a narrow rock ledge bordering the endless fields. Jules sits with her knees drawn tight to her chest. A faded, scavenged topographical map from one of the survival duffels is spread across her thighs. Her stiff, white-knuckled fingers struggle to keep the thin paper flat against the biting gale. With the blinding fog finally cleared, she traces the ink lines to the powerlines and jagged rock formations in the distance, desperate to establish an independent sense of direction away from their terrifying navigator.

Jaw grinding, she pushes her cloudy glasses up. The towering landmarks refuse to align with a single coordinate on the paper.

Ery steps over the ledge. Her clothes are heavily crusted with dried mud and chalky sediment. A fresh, dark scratch cuts a raw line across the right side of her cheek. Favouring the weak, trembling muscles in her right arm, she carefully lowers herself onto the cold stone beside Jules.

Using her left side, Ery leans in and pulls Jules flush against her rubs. She unfurls her wing, wrapping the thick silk tightly around the shivering woman.

With a small hitch in her focus, she leans her entire weight backwards into her warmth. Her free arm reaches up, absent-mindedly wrapping around Ery's waist.

The group weaves through the deep fields until the rolling grass gives way into a massive, terrifying gorge. The howling crosswind funnels aggressively up the sheer drop, threatening to peel them off the rock face. Spanning the abyss is a degraded, corroded transit bridge missing half of its panels. Suspended chest-high and running parallel to the catwalk, a single, heavy steel cable is bolted to a stone anchor, vibrating in the gale.

The stranger does not halt at the anchor, her boots planting securely on the narrow grating. She steps directly out over the abyss, leaving the outworlders and their massive survival duffels at the edge of the sunken earth.

Jules moves to the edge of the drop, her eyes tracking the vibrating cable as she calculates the tension of the bridge.

"We can't carry these across. We will get blown over the edge," she commands, her breath picking up a hitch beneath her coat. She points at the hefty bags resting in the grass, then to the suspended steel cable. "We can hoist them up, double-loop the canvas straps around the main line, then lock them in with the carabiners so we can push them across."

"I'll hoist the first one," Koa pants, his voice raw. He pushes a weak smile towards Jules. "I'm already standing at the anchor."

"Koa, your hands are shaking," Jules says, stepping toward him. "Let me tie it."

"It's just the cold. I've got it," Koa insists. Before she can intercept him, he reaches down and grabs the thick canvas straps of the nearest survival duffel.

He heaves the bag off the ground, straining to lift the dead weight chest-high toward the steel cable. The howling up-draft catches the canvas, dragging his boots dangerously close to the ledge. Sleep deprivation and the toxic infection degrade his fine motor control. Sweat begins to bead on his forehead as he desperately attempts to weave the strap over the rusted line. He fumbles the leaden carabiner with his bandaged arm.

The metal slips against the steel. The canvas strap snaps through his sweating palms.

The heavy survival bag plummets over the sheer edge, tearing past his boots. The massive weight is swallowed by the drop of the abyss.

Jules's faded topographical map slips from her fingers, tumbling over the edge and vanishing into the gorge alongside the survival gear. She does not reach for it.

"Twenty per cent of our caloric reserves. Filtering masks. A thermal blanket," Jules calculates aloud. She turns directly to Koa, stepping into his space. "You are physically compromised. The tissue in your arm is necrotic, and your fine motor skills are degraded. Your insistence on masking a physical deficit just cost us critical resources."

The smile collapses from his face. He stares down into the ink-black shadows of the gorge. Slowly, his raw, trembling hands drop to his sides.

The crossing is completed in a dead, suffocating silence.

They push into the fields. Hours bleed away with every step through the waist-high grass. Above them, the piercing azure sky darkens into a bruised, high-saturation violet, casting long, ink-black shadows across the rock formations as the outworlders watch their first sunset on the alien planet.

Koa drags his sneakers through the dirt. His breathing degrades into a wet, agonising rattle, echoing loudly. His ankle catches against a half-buried stone.

He crashes face-first into the dirt. His limbs go completely slack.

Before the dust even settles over his body, Jules and Ery plunge into the dirt. They throw themselves directly over Koa, their fingers digging fiercely into the fabric of his tattered jacket. Jules shields the boy's head with her own torso, her breathing shallow and ragged.

The guide halts. She turns, her pupils darting as she looks down at the pile of bodies in the crimson grass. She analyses the aggressive necrosis spreading beyond Koa's bandage and the critical failure of his motor functions. Her small, pale hands drop to her hip.

The tactical glaive unseats from its holster with a sharp, metallic ring.

Before she opens her mouth, Jules snaps her spine straight. Her boots grind against the dirt as she steps squarely into her space, physically placing herself between the monster and her fallen family. She uses every inch of her height, towering over the diminutive killer.

Her jaw lucks tight, her hands curling into fists at her sides. She stares straight down through her cloudy glasses, her upper lip peeling into a snarl.

"I don't care about your math. You touch him, and I will fucking kill you."

The stranger's hand pauses. Her eyes snap upward from the dying boy to Jules, her pupils dilating as she reads the spike in her heart rate, the aggressive tilt of her chin and the absence of self-preservation.

A twitch ripples through her wings.

She clicks her weapon back into its seating, taking a slow step back into the crimson grass, crossing her arms.

Minty's shoulders sag as the glaive disappears back into its holster. Her knees hit the dirt beside Koa. Her trembling hands reach out, gently peeling back the torn sleeve of his thermal coat. She checks the seal on the gauze, her eyes watering at the sight of the sickly, yellow necrosis spreading beneath the adhesive. Minty leans her head down, her ear hovering just inches over his shivering, rattling chest to listen to his lungs.

"You will be okay," Minty whispers softly, her voice barely carrying over the howling wind. "I promise."

You will be okay, I promise.

The wind stops.

The demi-human's head snaps towards the taur. Her four boots tear across the crimson grass, closing the distance in a blur. Before Jules can even track the speed, small pale hands lock on like vices onto the thick collar of Minty's winter coat. The guide physically hauls the taur backwards through the dirt. The impact knocks the air from Minty's lungs as her spine is slammed flush against a jagged, sun-bleached boulder.

"Get your hands off her!" Jules screams, her voice cracking raw as she lunges across the grass, her hands violently grabbing at the stranger's oversized coat to tear her away, but she refuses to budge.

The demi-human presses her arms against the boulder, her breathing reduced to erratic, hyperventilating gasps that echo off the stone.

"Why did you say that?" she demands, her voice frantically tearing through the wind. "If you say it, does his biology repair itself? Is it an audible trigger? Does it work!?"

Pinned against the sun-bleached boulder, Minty's breath hitches. Her shoulders drop as she looks down into the shorter girl's trembling eyes, watching her emotion bleed into the dying sunlight.

Minty's pulse slows. She stops pulling against the small, pale hands locking her collar to the stone.

"No, Cadence," Minty whispers.

The syllables hang over the rustling crimson grass. She holds the girl's desperate gaze.

Jules's grip on the coat freezes, her hands slowly, hesitantly loosening their hold on the shivering demi-human.

"It's just a lie we tell people we love so they aren't scared."

The designation hits the demi-human with physical force. The name strikes like a live wire against her nervous system.

The stranger's upper lip peels back over her teeth. A raw, aggressive snarl tears from her throat.

Her small hands go completely slack against the thick winter fabric. They slip uselessly from her collar, dropping to her sides. Her stare breaks, dropping numbly to the dirt beneath her boots.

Jules releases her grip and takes a step to the side, watching her movements intently.

Silent, she turns her back on the jagged boulder. Her boots drift aimlessly through the deep grass, her steps dragging sluggishly as she wanders in the general direction of their transit vector. She halts a dozen paces away, her silhouette shrinking against the bruised violet sky as she stares blankly over the darkening horizon.

Jules's brow furrows deeply behind her glasses. her hands drop to her sides. Slowly, she turns her back on the monster and kneels back into the dirt beside Koa's motionless body. Ery shifts her weight, her cardigan brushing against Jules's shoulder as the three outworlders huddle tightly around the collapsed boy.

"What did you just call her?" Jules asks, her knuckles gripping tightly against her knees.

Minty rubs her stinging collarbone. She looks past Jules's shoulder to the solitary figure staring into the dark.

"Cadence."

CHAPTER

Burnt Ash

Jagged spines of pale slate pierce the crust like splintered bone, stripping away the soft grass to leave a sprawling expanse of barren, broken stone. Tearing through the exposed ravines, a howling crosswind batters the outworlders, carrying the sharp, metallic scent of oxidised minerals and the dust of half-buried circuit boards lodged deep within the dirt.

Far ahead of the struggling group, Cadence ascends a near-vertical slab of exposed slate. Her four boots find fissures in the smooth stone, her taur-like lower half absorbing the sheer incline. She does not look back.

At the base of the slab, Minty's hooves scrape frantically against the stone. She lunges upward, attempting to follow the guide's exact path, but her keratin strikes zero traction on the incline. She slips backward with a sharp, terrified gasp, her frame crashing heavily into the chalky sediment at the bottom of the ravine.

Jules steps directly between the fallen taur and the towering cliff face.

"Do not follow her vector," Jule's voice cracks raw against the wind. She points her pen away from the sheer drop, slashing a horizontal line toward a longer, jagged switchback cutting through the rocks. "We take the lateral route."

Koa pushes himself off the stone wall, shifting two heavy survival duffels onto his good right shoulder. The sudden, localized mass throws his balance completely off. He stumbles sideways on his bad ankle, his shoulder colliding hard against Minty as she tries to stand.

"I'm sorry!" Minty gasps, her large ears pinning flat against her head. "I was in the way, I-"

"Minty, please stop apologising."

Jules marches to the vanguard, her fabric snapping violently around her knees in the gale. She jabs her pen directly at the slate.

"Step on the centre of the strata," Jules dictates, the sharp syllables clipping through the gale to combat the deafening roar of the air. She slashes the pen toward the next unbroken stone. "Keep your strides short. We cannot afford the caloric deficit of slipping."

Trailing behind the rear of the line, Ery favours her weak right arm, her boots dragging heavily across the uneven stone as she leans into the downdraft. Her amber eyes drift from the rigid, geometric path. Just beyond the marked track, the wind catches the brittle pages of a degraded, synthetic booklet lying half-buried lodged underneath a rusted oxygen canister.

Ery shifts her stride toward the discarded debris. Her heel catches the jagged lip of the slate, causing her to stumble forward with a sharp gasp as she drops to her knees to retrieve the faded manual.

Jules halts immediately. The sudden, rigid stop causes Minty and Koa to stumble awkwardly against each other on the narrow path. Far ahead, Cadence does not turn around, her four boots continuing their solitary, unyielding ascent up the mountain.

The metal pen snaps back, pointing directly at the designated, bare stone.

"Ery, get back on the path!" Jules snaps, her jaw locked tight against the biting wind. "We are operating on a severe caloric deficit. Stop wasting your energy on useless trash and stay in formation."

Ery's clutches her injured arm tighter against her chest, shrinking against the howling crosswind. Nodding at the ground, she quietly slips the torn manual into the pocket of her cardigan, dragging her boot back onto the hard slate.

The biting gale forces the outworlders to funnel into a scoured, narrow ravine, the towering slate walls offering a meagre reprieve from the crosswind. The brief halt is immediately broken by a steep, narrow step-up in the stone.

Koa drops his massive canvas duffels at the base of the incline. Dragging his good arm across his sweating forehead, Koa releases a strained breath and wedges his shoulder directly against the rock wall.

His knuckles bleach white as he aggressively grabs the thick canvas straps up the jagged ledge.

Minty's body is forced flush against the rock face to squeeze past the swinging duffels. The edge of the stone crumbles. Minty slips, her knees hitting the slate with a dull thud.

She scrambles upward instantly, physically pulling her thin winter coat tightly around her torso.

Ery steps past the shivering taur, her boots crunching over the loose rocks. Reaching down with her left hand, she grabs the thick canvas strap of Koa's second bag, throwing her weight backward to help him lift it over the jagged ledge. The weak, trembling muscles in her right shoulder give out completely under the strain.

The heavy canvas hits the dirt with a thud, kicking up a cloud of chalky dust that immediately scatters in the wind.

Jules crosses the slate, intercepting the moth-girl, the weight of her own bag shifting against her back. Her rigid posture slumps. She places her own hand firmly over the canvas strap.

"Drop it, Ery, your arm is compromised. You're a net negative on the lift and you're just getting in Koa's way. You can't help here."

Ery stares at Jules's hand resting on the hefty bag.

Her amber eyes drift away from the canvas strap.

Half-buried in the chalky sediment beside Jules's boots rests a shattered piece of rusted equipment.

The metal casing is cracked open, its internal wiring spilling uselessly into the dirt. A thick layer of abrasive grime coats the glass lens, blinding its sensors. It sits exactly where it was dropped ages ago, its function permanently degraded by the environment, left entirely behind by a crew that could no longer afford the caloric cost of carrying broken hardware through the storms.

Ery steps forward, her left-hand striking Jules squarely in the centre of her chest. The sudden impact forces the architect backwards. Jules stumbles across the uneven slate, her cloudy glasses slipping from the bridge of her nose to clatter against the hard stone and skid into the chalky dust.

Jules freezes. Her hands hover empty in the howling air.

Ery's chest heaves in jagged gasps. Tears spill over her cheeks, catching the wind and stinging the raw scratch on her face.

"You don't fucking care if I help!" Her airy voice splinters into a wet, shaking sob over the roaring air. "You just- you just want me to fit into your stupid, perfect little lines! You're not protecting us, Jules! You just boss us around because you're scared of the fucking dark! You use us!"

Choking on the thin air, Ery pivots. Minty's ears pin flat against her head, her shoulders shrinking back toward the rock face.

"And stop apologising!" Ery aims a trembling finger at the taur. "You just... you just say sorry for breathing so nobody ever holds you accountable for taking up space! You make yourself small so you don't have to deal with it!"

Her tear-streaked gaze cuts toward the ravine wall. Koa hunches there, clutching his bandaged arm against the stone as the gale whips his tattered sleeve.

"You're literally rotting, Koa," Ery gasps a breathless wheeze, her chest racking as she forces the words out. "But you won't drop the bags. You don't give a shit about protecting us... you just want us to beg you to stop! You just want us to tell you how useful you are! You're going to get us all fucking killed!"

The yelling echoes violently against the narrow, scoured walls of the ravine.

High above the bottleneck, perched motionless on a jutting shelf of oxidised slate, Cadence looks down at the fractured unit.

Four hefty boots strike the dirt as she drops into the centre of the clearing, the sharp crunch of her landing slicing through the silence. She steps directly into the space between Ery and the paralysed architect.

Cadence stares, unblinking, at Jules's blurred, unfocused eyes. "A command node driven by terror produces a statistical failure rate. Directives reliant on panic variables guarantee fatal deviations."

She pivots her mechanical posture toward Koa and Minty.

"Submissive behavioural routines implemented to avoid accountability create lethal blind spots in perimeter defence and team dynamics," the demi-human continues, her voice a flat, rapid stream of data over the wind. "Sacrificial actions born of a perceived utility deficit are statistically suicidal, masking a desire for validation rather than functional protection. Retaining a unit with necrotic tissue reduces transit efficiency. Emotional tethers generate fatal variables."

Cadence lowers her hands to her sides, her pupils sweeping over the exhausted, battered group.

"You are all fundamentally defective."

Jules remains paralysed in the dirt. Minty shrinks against the slate, and Koa stares blankly at his boots.

Ery's chest heaves. The moth-girl wipes the hot tears from her scratched cheek and steps directly toward the unblinking guide, her feathery antennae flaring outward in raw, uncoordinated fury.

"Stop treating us like broken machines!" Ery yells, her airy voice cracking as she points a trembling finger directly at the oversized researcher's coat. "You don't know anything about protecting a family! You just stand up there and judge us like you're some kind of perfect, untouchable commander! You're just a kid! How old are you even supposed to be!?"

She stares blankly at Ery's trembling finger.

"My chronological age is three hundred and forty-three years. My developmental stasis was terminated one thousand, four hundred and sixty-one days ago."

Ery stares blankly at Cadence's glare.

"My biological age is twelve."

The deafening howl of the crosswind tears through the barren stone.

The faded researcher's coat sweeps over the sediment as Cadence pivots on her boots, marching directly past the paralysed outworlders and resuming her mechanical ascent up the steep incline of the ravine.

Ery's hand shakes as she reaches into the pocket of her stained cardigan. Her fingers pull the torn, synthetic booklet free from the fabric. Her amber eyes pan from the retreating silhouette of the scarred monster scaling the rocks back down to the faded, stained cover in her palm. The bold, block lettering reads:

UNIT COHESION & PSYCHOLOGICAL WARFARE

Her trembling thumb flips the cover. The brittle, old pages immediately fracture under the pressure of her grip. The howling gale catches the dry rot. The paper crumples and flakes into tiny, ash-like pieces, tearing violently out of her hands and scattering into the sky. Ery lunges forward, her fingers swiping desperately at the empty air to catch the fleeing text, but the wind rips it away entirely.

Ery's knees buckle, hitting the abrasive slate. She buries her tear-streaked face deep into her trembling palms, her massive wings shuddering as she weeps into the dust.

Against the ravine wall, Koa stares at the two canvas duffels resting in the dirt. His jaw grinds.

Minty pulls the collar of her winter coat tightly over her head, tucking her tail flush against her hinds to shrink against the cold stone.

A few feet away, Jules remains on her hands and knees. Her bare fingers sweep blindly across the abrasive stone, searching the chalky sediment for her dropped glasses. Her hand brushes the metallic frame. She stops.

They lie sunken in the dirt.

CHAPTER

You're to Blame

High above the exposed stone, dense clouds gently roll across the sky, dimming the short-lived sunshine and slowly casting bruised shadows against the landscape. A howling crosswind rips through the ravines, carrying a distinct, damp scent of soaked leaves. The outworlders walk as isolated silhouettes, keeping vast, deliberate gaps between their shoulders, their eyes locked firmly on the ground to avoid acknowledging each other.

Ery's antennae twitch against the gale, catching the bitter shift in the atmosphere. She glances up from the loose rocks, looking past Koa's sluggish silhouette to seek out their guide. The diminutive girl stares fixedly ahead, her pupils wide as she tracks out a shifting shadow cast by a skeletal powerline in the distance. The rusted cables are connected to a sprawling structure wedged between two distant mountains. Ery parts her lips to speak, but seeing the unblinking fixation on Cadence's face, she swallows, tracing the outline of Jules's footprints instead.

At the base of the narrow ravine, Cadence halts, her four boots grinding to a stop against the shale. her chest hitches sharply, her eyes locked on the structure shadowing the valley floor ahead of them.

She pivots on her heels, the coat snapping in the wind as she turns her back on the wide, clear path leading through the facility perimeter. She begins to scale the highly unstable, thin pathway cutting up the side of the crumbling shale embankment.

Jules stops at the base of the incline, her chest heaving beneath her coat as she stares up at the sheer drop.

"Wait!" she yells over the howling crosswind, pointing towards the paved valley floor they are bypassing. "Why are we climbing that instead of going through the centre?"

Cadence does not pause her ascent. She does not look back at Jules or the pathway.

"The valley floor is a toxic sink," she drones, driving her boots deeper into the loose shale, spraying loose rocks down the incline. "Barometric pressure indicates the ozone is prone to pooling. It is dangerous to stay this low."

Jules looks from the smooth, roughly paved valley floor to the crumbling switchback. Feeling the first cold sweep in and the cold drops of moisture hitting her cheeks, she reluctantly pockets her hand.

The outworlders drag their exhausted bodies up the sheer face of the crumbling embankment. Sharp, loose rocks stab at their thermal coats with every inch. The scratch across the right side of Ery's face burns as she presses her chest flush against the stone, her stained skirt dragging heavily against the jagged incline. Minty's hard hooves scrape frantically for purchase just below her, the taur slipping backward with every step, forcing her to bury her chin deep into her thin winter coat to block out the howling wind.

Ery reaches her weak right arm upward, her fingers blindly searching for a stable outcropping. The trembling muscles in her shoulder completely give out.

Her fingers slip from the stone.

A gasp tears from her throat as gravity rips her off the rock face. Her massive teardrop wings thrash uselessly against the howling wind, her mud-drenched skirt catching the loose shale as she begins to slide rapidly toward the fatal, jagged drop-off at the base of the incline.

Koa lunges blindly upward from the narrow path below. The torn, bandaged sleeve of his thermal coat snaps violently in the gale as he throws his body weight forward into her trajectory. His raw hands clamp around Ery's waist. She desperately grabs at his wrists, trying to physically pry his strained fingers off her cardigan, but the sheer momentum of her fall instantly knocks his sneakers out from under him.

They both crash hard against the rock face, tumbling violently down the sharp incline. Koa's chest heaves with a wet cough, his knuckles bleaching white as he digs the heels of his sneakers and his good shoulder into the crumbling shale to break their descent. They slide to a heavy, breathless stop just inches from the sheer drop, fresh scrapes bleeding through their thermal gear.

Jules turns at the sound of the avalanche. Her chest hitches in a panicked gasp. Her boots finally clear the lip of the sheer climb, hitting the flat, solid rock of a wide switchback plateau. Behind her, Minty hauls herself over the ledge, her knees hitting the stone.

Jules scrambles up the loose shale, her glasses streaked with mild drops of condensation. She plants her boots directly in front of Cadence.

Looking past the monster, her gaze drops over the ridge to examine the "toxic sink" they had nearly died to avoid. She looks down at the perfectly intact transit highway cutting directly through the ravine, deeply sheltered by the crosswind and free of pooling ozone.

The valley floor isn't a hazard at all.

Jules's shoulders tighten. She looks back up at the rest of the lethal cliff face, then back down at Koa and Ery slowly pulling themselves off the rocks.

Jules whips her hand forward, pointing her finger directly at the scarred face of their guide. her chest heaves with a ragged breath.

"You lied," Jules hisses, her voice cracking over the howling wind. "There is no hazard down there. Why are we climbing this cliff?"

Cadence does not meet Jules's eyes.

Her unblinking stare remains fixedly locked on the powerlines strung high above the plateau. Her vocal cords continue to drone.

"Soil acidity is higher than average," she recites blindly. "Current wind velocity approaches terminal updraft.

The atmospheric particulate density-"

"I asked you a question!" Jules yells, stepping forwards.

"Atmospheric particulate indicates a rapid concentration of corrosive elements," the demi-human continues, her voice speeding up. "The valley floor creates a localized vacuum. Survival without immediate shelter-"

Jules closes the distance, her sneakers planting firmly on the loose shale, driving her directly into Cadence's personal space until her glasses are mere inches from the unblinking face.

"What is wrong with you, Cadence!?"

The raw volume of Jules's scream tears through the gale.

The stream of data dies in Cadence's throat. Her pupils contract to pinpricks as her breathing stops.

Her boots scramble frantically backwards across the shale, losing all traction. Her four legs folds underneath her. She collapses backwards against the cold stone of the ridge like a frightened foal.

She throws her small, pale hands tightly over the back of her neck, burying her face into her knees. Her wings flare outward in a sudden, defensive reflex, trembling violently against the rock face. She shrinks into the chalky sediment, her chest heaving.

Jules stops dead. Her posture completely sinks, dissolving into the shale. Their survival machine is a cowering child.

Her knees hit the chalky dust. She leans forwards, her glasses catching the trembling silhouette of the demi-human.

"Cadence..." she extends a shaking hand towards the huddled wings. "Who did that to you?"

Before the shivering girl can unbury her face, a sharp hiss strikes the back of Jules's exposed neck.

She flinches violently, her hand slapping against the sudden burn. Her gaze shoots upwards, her eyes snapping to the horizon. The bruised sky has blackened to a deep, crushing purple. The wind is cold, carrying bitter copper-tinted ozone directly into the outworlders' burning lungs. The first heavy drops of caustic rain begin to pound against the dry chemical sediment of the plateau.

Jules spins towards the shivering outworlders. Koa and Ery are pulling themselves off the stone whilst Minty's large ears are pinned flat in terror against the sudden shift in atmospheric pressure.

"Koa! Ery! Move back down to the floor of the valley now!" she yells over the rising thunder, before turning to Minty. "You have to help me move Cadence."

The guide remains catatonic in the dirt. Jules drops back to her knees, gently but firmly wrapping her arms around Cadence's shoulders to pull her upwards.

Minty lunges through the biting wind, her hooves scrambling across the damp shale. She wraps her arms under Cadence's elbows. They drag the catatonic, hyperventilating demi-human back down the crumbling, lethal cliff face.

Toxic rain pounds against their coats, dissolving the chalky sediment into a slick, burning sludge. The downdraft pushes against them as they retrace their precarious steps back toward the wide transit highway.

Reaching the flat valley floor, the immense shadow of the structure Cadence had been so desperate to avoid swallows the outworlders. Jules drags her glasses across her sleeve, her eyes sweeping the towering, brutalist concrete wall built directly into the side of the mountain. At the exact centre of the stone foundation, directly beneath the massive, skeletal powerline anchored to the roof, sits a pair of leaden, oxidised iron blast doors.

"Over here!" Jules screams, releasing Cadence into Minty's grip. She bounds forwards and throws her entire body weight against the rusted seal. The metal refuses to yield.

Koa's torn sneaker hits the pavement beside her, his good shoulder slamming into the iron. Ery presses her weak, trembling hands against the seam. With their desperate combined strength, the leaden doors grind open with an agonizing shriek of ancient steel, breaking the old vacuum seal with a rush of caustic air.

They all squeeze through the gap in the door, spilling into the pitch-black corridor, the howling storm whistling behind them.

Jules produces her high-lumen flashlight from her belt. The harsh beam pierces the dark, illuminating a strong, sterile tunnel of cracked white tile.

The outworlders and Cadence drag their feet down the corridor. The flashlight beam sweeps over carts of brutalist, corroded medical equipment on trolleys pushed against the walls. Thick, stained-glass observation windows look into empty, sterile rooms. The light glints on the deep black scorch marks scarring the concrete walls, then drops to illuminate corroded iron restraints bolted to the arms and legs of rigid surgical chairs. Cadence's eyes are locked to the tiles as she wheezes under the sound of everyone's damp footsteps.

The end of the medical corridor opens into a sprawling, cluttered archive library.

Cadence's boots do not wait for the beam to sweep the room. Her hands fly up to grip the collar of her faded researcher's coat, her entire frame scrambling blindly away from the scattered medical trays and rusted restraints. She retreats rapidly into the deepest, darkest corner of the archive library, curling her four legs tightly beneath her and burying her head into her knees. Ery flinches backward at the sudden movement, her gaze tracking the hyper-lethal guide shrinking into the shadows like a cornered animal.

The outworlders collapse against the nearest walls, their chests heaving with ragged, wet coughs in the stale air. Jules strips off her coat, shaking the caustic rain from the fabric with a snap before tossing it across a long, granite table.

Her flashlight beam tracks across the pristine, unweathered room. Preserved by the iron airlock, the geometric insignia they had seen bleeding in the mud is perfectly intact. The logo is stamped across scattered paperwork, stationery and painted in massive, faded block letters across the far concrete wall.

Axiom.

Jules draws in a deep, unstable breath, clamping the cold metal of her flashlight tightly between her teeth. She throws herself at the long granite table,

her shaking hands clawing through the scattered paperwork and scanning the labels on the steel cupboards lining the walls.

The bright beam sweeps across the stark pages. There's no map here.

Jules's hands freeze over a collection of filed dossiers, clipped with glossy medical polaroids and thick, rolled physical schematics. The unredacted heading "Accelerated Evolution Trials" is stamped across every document. The flashlight shakes in her jaw as she illuminates a massive blueprint detailing the surgical grafting of skeletal wing structures. Beneath the schematics are high-resolution photographs of catastrophic chemical burns.

The glossy pages slip from her fingers. The flashlight clatters loudly against the granite table, rolling off the edge and hitting the tile floor with a sharp crack.

The beam rolls across the sterile floor, illuminating the rusted restraints in the hallway, and finally coming to rest on the shivering, scarred silhouette of Cadence hiding in the pitch-black corner.

The immense space of the library is amplified by the howling shriek of the toxic storm tearing against the iron airlock at the end of the medical corridor.

Koa has completely given out, lying motionless on a thermal blanket retrieved from one of his duffels, his chest heaving in an unsteady rhythm. Ery sits beside him, wedged into a sleeping bag, clutching her injured right arm. From the darkest, furthest corner of the library, Cadence remains unnervingly still, the unblinking eyes of the guide tracking the outline of every structure on the sterile tiles.

Jules paces the length of the tunnel leading to the bulky blast doors. She furiously shoves a heavy, rusted surgical cart directly against the iron seal. Her glasses dart frantically from the dark corners of the observation windows to the dead airlock, her hands shaking as she stacks another rusted tray onto the barricade. Minty hovers a few feet away, watching Jules obsessively attempt to physically seal out the horrors of the facility.

"Minty," Jules commands, speaking over a faded strike of thunder. She points at a massive, overturned steel cabinet. "Bring that here. Now, please."

Minty's hands tremble as she grips the edge of the thick steel. She heaves, but finds no traction on the slick, unnatural tile of the laboratory. They scrape and slide, a clatter of keratin against smooth ceramic echoing through the library as the massive cabinet refuses to budge.

"I-I can't," she gasps, her chest heaving as she drops her grip, leaning against the metal.

Jules spins around, glaring at the exhausted taur.

"You are leaving the perimeter exposed," She points her fingers at the rusted blast doors whistling under the storm. "We cannot secure the airlock if you don't move it. Ery is severely injured and Koa is practically comatose. You are the only one with the mass to move it."

Minty shrinks under the harsh fluorescent beam of the flashlight Jules grips tightly beneath white knuckles.

"I'm trying, Jules. My hooves just can't catch on the floor, It's-"

"Then find leverage!"

Jules yells. The volume tears through the echoing chamber.

Minty physically recoils backward across the slick sterile tile, wrapping her arms tightly around her torso. She looks down.

"Jules… please," Minty whispers shakily.

Tears spill over her cheeks, cutting through the ash and chalk dust streaking her face. Her voice sounds broken.

"I'm so sorry. I know you're scared. I want to make things better, but I can't- I can't make things better."

The metallic glare of Jules's flashlight shivers in her grip.

Minty braces, squeezing her eyes shut, before turning away, scrambling backward into the library. She pulls the collar of her coat tightly over her head as she shrinks into the dark.

The harsh beam of the flashlight trembles violently against the empty tiles where Minty had just stood.

Jules lowers the light, the beam rolling weakly across the rusted blast doors, the light casting a line of light through the sky through it. The metal refuses to lock perfectly flush. A thin, jagged silver of freezing, caustic air from the toxic storm howls through the compromised seal, biting sharply against

Jules's exposed neck.

She stares at the gap.

Her knees hit the cold, sterile ceramic floor. She sinks back into the brutalist concrete of the medical corridor, her spine sliding down the wall until she is seated in a pitch-black corner beside the door, her hands shake so severely she cannot hold the polymer casing of the flashlight. It slips from her fingers, clattering onto the tile and rolling to a stop, casting long, distorted shadows across the abandoned surgical carts.

A violent, blinding flash of lightning tears through the narrow crack in the iron doors.

The deafening, concussive crack of thunder follows, rattling the floorboards.

Jules draws her knees tightly to her chest. She wraps her arms around her shins, burying her face deep into her pants.

She shudders, weeping alone in the dark.

CHAPTER

10

Terrible Walks of Life

Pale, bruised sunlight bleeds through the thick glass of a small observation dome, refracting across the white-tiled corridor.

The toxic storm has ceased, leaving a stillness trapped within the walls. The air inside the subterranean bunker sits stagnant in the lungs, choked with the sharp, metallic bite of rusted iron and the stinging, old ghost of industrial antiseptic.

Jules stands within the dome, her chin tilted upward toward the clearing sky. The dark grooves beneath her cloudy glasses remain completely untouched by sleep.

A hallway away, the outworlders quietly pack their salvaged gear.

They are gathered around their few remaining supplies. Minty pulls the final, dry ration block and a half-empty water canister from the third duffel bag. She turns the bag inside out, shaking the last of the chalky crumbs onto the floor before folding the now-empty canvas and cinching it to the side of her own pack.

They work single-handedly, using their free hands to gnaw on minuscule, rigidly divided blocks of synthetic rations. Koa hisses as he yanks the heavy canvas straps of his two duffels tight over his freshly bandaged arm. Minty's hooves click softly against the sterile tiles, locking her gaze firmly on the ground. Beside the taur, Ery bites her bottom lip, dragging her trembling, right arm through the thick sleeve of her thermal coat.

Jules steps out of the observation dome, her sneakers squeaking across the clinical tiles as she retreats back into the medical archive. She sinks against the edge of the long granite table. Her cloudy glasses are thickly smudged with chalky sediment and the dried tracks of tears from the night before. Her unblinking gaze fixes blankly on the blueprints scattered across the cold tile.

At the far end of the corridor, Cadence stands, her back pressed flush against the rusted blast doors. Her pale fingers grip the collar of her oversized researcher's coat, pulling the synthetic fabric as tightly as possible against her small, shivering frame as she stares at the thin sliver of morning light seeping through the cracked airlock.

The oversized sleeve rides up her arm, revealing a deep, jagged scrape carved violently across Cadence's pale forearm. It was a fresh, bleeding laceration from her collapse on the switchback plateau the day before.

The raw edges of the wound are crusted thick with the abrasive chalk sediment of the Highlands.

Jules's eyes shift from her injured arm to the horrific medical polaroids of melted skin and skeletal grafting. She pushes her cloudy glasses up the bridge of her nose, reaching into her canvas bag, her fingers quietly unzipping a medical kit.

The outworlders pause their packing, their eyes darting up from their bags.

Jules halts a few paces away from the guide, intentionally giving her a wide perimeter. She draws out a long exhale, her shoulders sinking.

"You're bleeding," Jules whispers, gently extending her open hand, displaying the clean, white roll of bandages on her palm. She bends her knees, slowly lowering herself into a crouch until she is perfectly eye-level with the shivering girl. "The dust is going to make it fester. Just let me clean it for you before we leave."

A tall figure wrapped in a coat. Holding sterile medical supplies. Speaking with soft gentleness inside a laboratory.

Just let me clean it for you before we leave.

"Let me clean it for you."

"The burning means the graft is holding."

"I know it hurts, little bird. But the residue is going to make it fester."

"I can still run."

"I know you can. But you have to let me wrap it before we leave. Let me hide it for you."

...before we leave.

Her four boots scramble erratically against the cracked tile, and a pale arm snaps outward with blinding speed.

She violently slaps the pristine roll of sterile gauze out of Jules's outstretched palm.

The white bandage hits the cold ceramic floor with a hollow smack. It unspools rapidly across the tiles, trailing a long, clean line of fabric until the roll strikes the rusted iron leg of a stained surgical chair.

Cadence's spine crashes hard backward into the leaden iron blast doors, sealing her into the corner of the airlock. Her taur-like lower half completely folds beneath her as she sinks to the floor. She glares at Jules, eyes shivering, bracing her scarred body against the wall.

Jules freezes on her knees. Her cloudy glasses reflect the hyperventilating child backed against the airlock.

Her knees push off the floor. She turns her back on the cowering guide. Her shoulders slump deeply beneath her coat as she walks back to the long granite table.

Jules heaves her heavy canvas duffel over her shoulder. Koa, Minty, and Ery watch as Jules walks past the scattered medical polaroids. She reaches the airlock, hauling a rusted surgical cart and a pile of overturned steel trays away from the cracked seal. Tossing the barricade aside, she throws her weight against the unsealed iron doors, forcing them wide open and pulling the soft, freezing breeze of the Highlands back into the corridor.

High above the towering, skeletal powerlines, the violent purple bruises of the storm have completely faded into a vast, piercingly clear sky. The final twinkling stars dissolve silently into the bleeding, dark pink light of an early sunrise, casting long, soft shadows across the flat, paved expanse of the valley floor. An iridescent dew coats the long blades of the deep crimson grass pushing aggressively up through the cracked concrete, catching the dawn light.

Stepping through the rusted threshold, the outworlders stream out of the brutalist, subterranean facility and back into the freezing Highlands.

The air is sharp and brutally cold. Every ragged, exhausted exhale from the group plumes into a thick cloud of foggy condensation that dissipates in the morning chill.

Jules does not lead the march. She trudges listlessly behind Minty. The taur nervously clutches the collar of her winter coat, her hard hooves stepping reluctantly behind the unbothered silhouette of Cadence at the vanguard.

The shattered ferrocrete of the valley floor gives way to a sprawling, flat expanse of ankle-high crimson grass, dissolving into a wide, heavily rutted dirt path cutting a transit line directly toward the peaks. As the outworlders drag their shoes over the uneven ground, the rising orange sun casts their long shadows across the endless red field.

The dirt path is a graveyard.

The petrified debris of a panicked, catastrophic evacuation chokes the trail. Half-buried in the chalky sediment and crimson grass are the twisted, oxidised chassis of massive Axiom transport rovers left entirely to dissolve in the elements, surrounded by thousands of shattered oxygen canisters and split, synthetic luggage bags bleaching in the high-altitude sun.

Cadence's boots lock obsessively into the exact, petrified tyre tracks carved deep into the dirt. Her unblinking stare fixes blankly onto a crushed transport rover directly ahead.

The outworlders funnel into a wide clearing choked with the crushed, oxidised remains of three rovers, collapsing for a brief halt.

Jules pushes past the group, her cloudy glasses sweeping the debris field. She drops to her knees in the chalky dirt beside a massive, half-buried synthetic suitcase. Her hands shake from severe sleep deprivation and hunger. Her raw fingers claw uselessly at the petrified latches, unable to force the rusted steel to yield.

Crack.

With a sharp, concussive blow, Minty brings a rusted iron wrench she had scavenged from the mangled undercarriage of a nearby wreck down hard against the petrified suitcase.

The rusted lock shatters into jagged shrapnel.

Jules flinches violently backward, throwing her hands over her face against the sudden impact. Minty's large ears instantly pin flat against her skull as she drops the wrench.

"I'm sorry," Minty gasps, her voice a panicked rush.

"Did it hit you? I didn't mean to-"

"No," Jules interrupts, lowering her hands. She looks up at

the taur, her chest heaving. "No. I'm okay. Thank you, Minty."

Jules turns back to the suitcase. She forces the bulky synthetic lid open. Her white-knuckled fingers dig desperately into the preserved contents.

There are no emergency med-kits. She does not find filters or survival rations.

Jules pulls out a meticulously folded, civilian dress. Beneath the fine fabric rests a delicate, porcelain teacup, carefully packed beside a collection of glossy, physical family photographs. A faded, geometric insignia identical to the one on the medical archive doors is stamped across the corner of a cream document folder.

Jules's shaking hands pick up the top photograph. Her cloudy glasses reflect a perfectly preserved, smiling researcher in a lab coat holding a human toddler on a manicured lawn.

Her jaw clenches, grinding against the ozone. Carefully, lovingly packed suitcases with luxury, personal belongings.

Jules's fingers go numb. The glossy photograph slips from her grasp, landing face-up in the chalky dirt. The final, remnants of her rigid posture dissolve. She sinks backward until her spine hits the rusted chassis of a dead rover, staring blankly at the smiling faces.

Monsters.

A harsh, metallic crunch breaks the silence a few feet away.

Koa drags his sneakers through the crimson grass, his bad ankle buckling as his boot catches against a half-buried transport cooler. The rusted latch completely snaps under his weight. The impact violently kicks up the dust, spilling several pristine, vacuum-sealed freshwater containers across the dry sediment.

Koa drops to his knees beside the spill. His fingers freeze over a bright, tubular, vacuum-packed tubular foil pouch wedged tightly between the heavy canisters.

He pulls the reflective foil free from the dirt. The bandage on his arm pulls taut as he twists his wrists, forcing the thick seal to crack open.

A soft, overwhelmingly sweet and fragrant scent immediately bleeds into the freezing air.

Koa stares into the pouch. Inside is an intact scientifically preserved orange fruit, engineered purely for taste and comfort long before Fermata's natural flora had mutated. The moisture glistens against the foil, entirely untouched by the three hundred years of decay outside the vacuum seal.

Jules looks up from the dirt. Her cloudy glasses reflect the bright flash of the foil pouch in Koa's hands.

Sugary fruit possesses zero caloric utility or defensive value.

Jules pushes her glasses up the bridge of her nose. Her gaze sweeps slowly from the gleaming foil, past the scattered, abandoned equipment littered in the clearing to the shivering, exhausted faces of her family.

We aren't going to survive like them.

Jules pushes her sneakers off the rusted rover. She stands up in the howling wind and crosses the slate, her hands shivering. She gently takes the open foil pouch from Koa's raw fingers.

With a soft snap, Jules breaks the tubular, brightly coloured fruit into three perfectly even pieces.

She turns to Ery, pressing the first fragrant slice directly into the moth-girl's trembling left hand.

"I'm sorry," Jules whispers over the gale. She nods toward the scattered civilian luggage in the dirt. "We are not going to survive like them."

Jules turns her back on the photographs. She steps toward Koa, placing her hand gently on his uninjured shoulder to steady his buckling knees. She presses the second piece into his palm. "You don't have to carry us," Jules murmurs.

She steps toward the shivering taur, offering her open palm to Minty. "You don't have to apologise for needing this," Jules says softly, placing the final piece of fruit into Minty's hands.

Jules lowers her empty hands to her sides.

Ery and Minty stare down at the fragrant fruit resting in their palms. The overwhelming scent of sugar cuts sharply through the high-altitude ozone. Tears immediately prick Ery's amber eyes as she looks back up at the starving, hollowed girl.

Ery's weak right arm twitches as she reaches out with her left hand. She snaps her minuscule portion of the fruit in half and presses the soft, brightly coloured piece firmly back into Jules's empty palm.

Koa mirrors Ery, snapping his own ration and sliding it into Jules's fingers. Minty immediately follows suit, her shoulders dropping their tension.

They lean their heavy, exhausted shoulders against one another in the dust, quietly chewing the incredibly sweet fruit.

High atop the rusted cargo hold of a dead Axiom transport rover, Cadence blinks and snaps her gaze towards the outworlders.

The potent, fragrant scent of the engineered sugar drifts upward on the gale.

Jules looks up from the dirt. Through her cloudy glasses, she catches the wide, unblinking stare of the diminutive guide perched on the rover.

Jules pushes off the slate. Her boots crunch against the chalky sediment as she crosses the perimeter, climbing halfway up the rusted cargo hold. She extends her hand upward, holding out a tiny, final piece of the brightly coloured preserved fruit to the scarred demi-human.

Cadence stares at the soft, sugary ration. Her small, pale fingers twitch against her faded researcher's coat.

Very slowly, the trembling hand reaches out. Her fingers brush Jules's palm, snagging the tiny piece of fruit.

The second the sugar touches her skin; Cadence violently jerks backward. Her four boots scramble erratically across the rusted metal roof of the rover.

She clutches the tiny piece of preserved fruit tightly against her chest, turning her back on the outworlders. She throws herself off the far side of the transport, rushing blindly to hide behind the rusted, oxidised chassis where the defective variables cannot see her.

Jules's hand hangs empty over the edge of the rover. The outworlders stand silent, exchanging bewildered glances as the she physically flees with a piece of fibrous sugar.

Hidden completely behind the rusted metal, out of sight of the howling wind and the fractured family, Cadence's knees buckle.

Her lower half folds beneath her as she sinks into the chalky dust. With both her shaking, pale hands, she carefully places the bright fruit onto her tongue. The overwhelmingly sweet, familiar taste instantly melts her form.

Cadence collapses forward, her head hitting her knees as she hugs her own waist tightly, rocking in the dirt.

CHAPTER

11

Someone, Somewhere, Somehow

The crimson grass bleeds away.

As they drag their feet upward, the steep incline of the horizon actively bleeds the vibrant colour from the landscape. The waist-high red grass thins out, turning brittle and sparse, until the vegetation is swallowed entirely by vast expanses of pale, exposed dirt and jagged slate.

A thin, creeping layer of frost begins to choke the sharp rock formations bordering the trail. Stripped of the dense ozone of the valley, the howling crosswind drops rapidly in temperature, the frigid air biting viciously through the heavy synthetic fabric of the outworlders' thermal coats. Jules's breath plumes into thick clouds of foggy condensation that freeze instantly against the lenses of her cloudy glasses as she looks down at the dirt.

Half-buried in the creeping permafrost lies a twisted, petrified skeleton.

The remains have been entirely scoured by centuries of the biting highland winds, but the horrific, unnatural architecture of the "Accelerated Evolution" subject is undeniable. A stunted, fragile human torso is grafted onto a small, taur-like lower half. Thick, fused bone joints jut violently from the spine where massive wings once rested. The skeleton is an exact mirror of their guide.

Driven deep into the freezing sediment directly beside the fragile skull stands a rusted, heavily oxidised metal pole. Tied tightly to the iron is a severely frayed, colourless ribbon of fabric. The ragged scrap snaps against the gale, a makeshift, desperate marker placed in the dirt long ago.

Jules raises a trembling hand, pushing her frosted glasses up the bridge of her nose.

"I found the blueprints," Jules whispers.

Koa, Minty, and Ery fix their eyes on Jules's face.

"They, or rather 'Axiom' called it 'Accelerated Evolution,'" Jules says, as she forces the words out into the freezing air. "I read the logs. The surgical grafting. The chemical burns."

Jules looks down at the fused joints of the skeleton in the dirt, her voice cracking.

"They treated them like hardware," Jules gasps softly. "Chemical burns. Oxygen deprivation. They forced every single one of her siblings through trials before discarding them as defective, useless variables. She's still here, somehow."

Far out of the acoustic range of the conversation, Cadence stands on an isolated rock outcropping of the ridge. Her boots pace in a rapid, agitated circle across the frost-choked slate. She keeps her back turned to the mummified remains.

Her vision darts back down at the outworlders. They are expending critical caloric reserves, halting the necessary transit speed, and actively risking severe hypothermia simply to stand in the freezing crosswind and stare at expired, useless biomass.

The number of calories they would waste if I died.

From her elevated perch, she sees Jules slowly bow her head. Minty's hand trembles as she gently places it over her own heart. Koa drops to his good knee, his knuckles white as he carefully, meticulously clears a jagged piece of loose slate away from the rusted marker pole.

Cadence's breath catches in her throat.

They would waste calories if I died.

Her hands drop limply to her sides, the heavy researcher's coat snapping wildly around her motionless silhouette as she stares down at the grieving family.

The drop in atmospheric pressure drags heavily against their lungs.

Jules sweeps her large flashlight across the clearing ahead of them, the beam of light cutting through the dense absence of light in the dusk.

Cadence wheezes against the freezing, high-altitude sky. She begins pacing in tiny, frantic circles at the head of the line, her small hands trembling.

Ery trails closely behind Jules, her feathery antennae twitching anxiously as she watches the erratic stumbles of the scarred girl.

"Should we rest?" Ery asks softly, her airy voice catching in the thin atmosphere. "She can't breathe."

She spins around, her four boots slipping against the ice, her chest heaving as she points a shaking, pale finger directly at the moth's chest.

"We have to keep moving!" Cadence wheezes, sweeping her gaze across the spread of outworlders. "I… am… your… designated guide… Our route is clear!"

Pushing her cloudy glasses up the bridge of her nose, Jules moves towards Koa and unclips both canvas bags from his waist.

They both hit the slate with a loud thud.

"We are resting,"

Koa limps directly past the protesting guide. His boots stop at the edge of the clearing, his jaw set as he stares out over the vast, barren expanse of jagged slate, planting his body directly on the perimeter line.

Minty's hooves cross to the opposite flank. She sinks heavily against a jagged boulder, curving her spine to construct a physical windbreak against the wind. Behind the taur's shelter, Jules kneels into the chalky dust, counting out remaining rations while Ery strikes a pale, smokeless chemical fire into life.

Cadence gasps, her pupils dilating wildly as she scrambles toward Koa's back. "I am the guard! If I do not-"

Ery steps forward, the hem of her stained skirt brushing the creeping frost. Reaching out with both hands, she gently wraps her soft, warm fingers securely around Cadence's freezing, violently trembling hands, physically halting her frantic pacing.

Cadence tries to jerk backward, her chest heaving desperately.

"I am the optimal guard," Cadence gasps as she pulls against Ery's grip. "I can maintain perimeter parameters. I can output utility,"

"You haven't slept since we fell here," Ery says, exerting a gentle downward pressure, slowly pulling the shivering guide into the dirt beside the chemical fire. "You have to rest."

"I do not require prolonged shutdown! I am designed for continuous transit!"

"You're twelve," Ery whispers softly. "Go to sleep."

Cadence's boots scrape weakly against the frost as she sinks into the chalky dirt, glaring up at the moth.

She looks past Ery's shoulder, her eyes darting wildly around the tiny camp.

Koa stands resolute against the barren drop-off, gripping his injured arm while scanning the dark. Minty's, shivering back completely blocks the biting wind. Jules sits up against a low boulder, her cloudy glasses reflecting the gentle fire.

Her taur-like lower half folds rigidly beneath her in the dust, her spine perfectly straight. Her heterochromatic pupils dart frantically from Koa's silhouette to Minty's back. Her fingers twitch against her knees.

Only the howling crosswind and the soft, steady crackle of the chemical fire respond to her vigilance.

Her unblinking glare begins to flutter.

The rapid hitching of her chest slowly smooths into a long breath.

The warmth of the fire seeps into her frozen skin.

Her chin drops a fraction of an inch, then jerks back up as she fights the crushing fatigue.

Now is not the time to sleep.

I have to get up.

I have to…

…

"89."

"Terminated."

"90."

"Terminated."

"91."

"Terminated."

"92."

"Functional. Barely."

"Pack it with the heavy equipment."

Cadence's eyes snap open.

The sky is a bruised purple of the highland morning.

She looks down. Meticulously wrapped around her small frame is Jules's warm utilitarian coat.

She sits up slowly, the thick fabric slipping over her shoulders.

To her right, Minty and Koa sit. Koa rubs his bandaged arm, a weak smile cracking his chapped lips.

"It wasn't even the rain that was the worst part," Koa says quietly, his voice hoarse from the thin air. "It was the slick asphalt on the delivery route. You'd hit the brakes on the scooter, and it felt exactly like sliding across this sediment. Complete loss of traction."

Minty's large ears swivel toward him. "Did you ever drop a delivery?" she asks softly.

"Only once," Koa chuckles, the sound catching in his throat. "A massive stack of pizzas right into a storm drain. I don't know how that happened, either."

On the opposite flank, Jules sits still, her back towards the smoking chemical fire, her cloudy glasses catching the early light. Ery leans against her, the moth-girl's feathery antennae fluttering in the gentle morning breeze.

"The ozone here is just so sterile," Ery hums, her amber eyes scanning the barren peaks. "It burns. On Earth, when a thunderstorm rolls in, it's messy and unpredictable, but it smells like wet soil and petrichor. It feels alive."

Jules stares longingly at the valley far below where they had come from. "Yeah, I miss it. You don't know what you have until it's gone, kind of thing."

Cadence sits still between the two pairs.

Her pale fingers brush the thick wool of Jules's coat draped over her lap.

Act 3

Chapters 12 - 16

CHAPTER

12

A Bag of Blood and Bones

Massive inclines of monolithic grey stone pierce the frost line.

The biting crosswind dies into a suffocating stillness. A continuous, gentle snowfall drifts through the void, blanketing the exposed rock in a pristine layer of snow.

Jules halts her march. Sweat streaks the inside of her cloudy glasses. She squeezes her hands into tight fists, driving her fingernails into her palms to anchor her swaying balance.

Behind her, Ery stumbles. Her boots drag through the fresh powder. A bright stream of blood drips from her nose, splashing starkly against the snow and soaking into the thick collar of her thermal coat.

Ery's amber eyes widen. Her hands fly to her face, her fingertips coming away smeared with red. Her feathery antennae pin flat against her skull as she releases shallow gasps.

Jules steps back through the snow. She wraps her hand firmly around Ery's uninjured arm.

"It is the altitude pressure," Jules breathes, the syllables catching in the thin air. "Our capillaries are bursting. Expect more blood the higher we climb. Keep your chin down."

"Am I bleeding out?" Ery whispers, her voice trembling slightly over the falling snow as she presses her ruined sleeve against her face. "Is it going to stop?"

The crunch of heavy canvas hitting the snowpack breaks the conversation.

The two survival duffels slip uselessly from Koa's good shoulder, the dead weight driving him forward.

He hacks violently, a thick splatter of dark, infected fluid staining the pristine white powder beside his boots. He attempts to lock his knees, but the muscles buckle completely under the severe hypoxia.

Koa crashes face-first against the hard, snow-dusted slate.

His limbs go limp.

The coat slips from Jules's shoulders as she drops her canvas bag into the snow. She lunges across the powder, her sneakers sliding wildly against the frosted stone until her knees hit the icy slate beside him.

He lies feverish and entirely unresponsive in a deep semi-coma, his skin slick with a cold, toxic sweat from the aggressively spreading yellow spore infection.

Her hands shake violently in the freezing air as she desperately digs through her collapsed coat, ripping open the canvas zipper of her medical kit. She presses two trembling fingers hard against the side of his neck, her voice cracking as she loudly counts out the fading thud of his pulse.

"...he's tachycardic," Jules gasps out, her cloudy glasses fogged with sweat. She unspools the remaining roll of sterile gauze. "His capillaries are blowing."

She aggressively rewraps his festering arm, forcing his head back against the snowpack, prying his eyelids open to check his unresponsive pupils.

The blood continues to seep through the fresh, white bandages. Koa's chest barely rises against the freezing stone. Jules's fingers dig desperately into the sides of his head, her voice breaking into a raw pitch as she tries to aggressively shake him back into consciousness.

"Koa, wake up!" She drops the useless roll of gauze, her hands clawing frantically at his thermal coat. "Listen to me! Your heart rate is failing! You have to wake up!"

Minty's hard hooves crunch softly through the powder.

Stepping directly over Koa's motionless body, Minty plants herself firmly in the snow, physically placing her chest between Jules and the dying boy.

Minty drops to her knees in the freezing dust. She gently reaches out, wrapping her warm hands securely around Jules's shaking wrists.

"Jules," Minty whispers.

Delicate, pristine snowflakes drift down, catching in Minty's hair and melting against her cheeks as she looks down at the scattered, blood-soaked gauze in the snow.

"He's dying."

Jules stares down at Koa. The bright, fresh blood from his nose continues to pool steadily into the clean powder beside his ear. His lips are a terrifying, sickly blue against the frost. The yellow, necrotic spore burn has swollen aggressively past the edges of the sterile gauze, weeping dark fluid onto his tattered sleeve.

"I can..." Jules whispers, her voice a thin, cracked wheeze over the falling snow. She tries to pull her hands free from the taur's grip, her cloudy glasses darting desperately toward the useless, scattered medical supplies. "If I..."

She looks from the soaking red gauze back to Koa's unresponsive, sunken eyes.

Jules's white-knuckled fingers go completely slack within Minty's grip.

Her chest heaves with a sudden sob. Jules falls forward, pulling Koa's limp, feverish upper body out of the snow and tightly into her lap. She buries her face deep into his mud-stained coat. The cloudy glasses press hard against his shoulder as she violently weeps, her shoulders shaking uncontrollably against the freezing stone.

The ragged, echoing sobs drift across the high-altitude pass, carrying through the continuous, gentle snowfall. Just a dozen paces ahead, Cadence stops.

She stands alone on an incline of grey stone, her four boots planted in the powder. She slowly turns back to face the group, her pupils widening against the bright, snowy glare as she processes the scene below her.

His biological mass is in active, fatal failure. To preserve the caloric reserves of the remaining group and optimise transit efficiency before the cold kills them all, the only statistically viable option is to abandon the dead weight.

Cadence stares at Jules's shaking shoulders. She looks at Minty's silent form kneeling protectively in the snow, and Ery clutching her bleeding nose, her amber eyes fixed on the dying boy.

A sharp, physical twitch ripples through the claws at the high point of Cadence's wings.

She stares at the family huddled in the freezing dirt.

Cadence's jaw locks tight. She turns away from the peak, her boots crunching slowly back down the snow-packed slate toward the outworlders.

As she closes the distance to their perimeter, she reaches deep inside the oversized researcher's coat. Her small fingers plunge into a concealed, heavily stitched pocket sewn into the inner lining. Her arm trembles as she carefully unearths a slender, matte-black metallic cylinder. A faded, universal medical insignia is etched into the casing above the glass chamber, which houses a dense, iridescent crimson fluid.

Her boots slide awkwardly against the frosted stone, her steps hesitant as she breaches the circle.

Cadence halts directly over Jules. She stares down at the architect burying her face into Koa's tattered jacket. Slowly, Cadence extends her pale hand outward, the sharp, metallic needle of the syringe gripped between her fingers.

The sob catches in Jules's throat. She rips her face away from the tattered coat.

Her tear-streaked, cloudy glasses snap upward, instantly catching the distorted reflection of the towering, scarred monster looming directly over Koa. The harsh glare of the snowfield flashes off the sharp, gleaming metallic needle gripped tightly in Cadence's trembling hands.

Jules's eyes lock onto the hardware.

Her jaw sets into a rigid line. She gently places Koa's feverish head down against the freezing, snow-packed stone, shielding his face from the falling powder.

Jules lunges forward from the frozen slate. Her sneakers slip against the fresh powder, throwing her entire body weight forward. Her fist connects with the side of the demihuman's jaw.

A sharp, wet crack echoes over the peaks.

The unexpected, violent impact whips Cadence's face sideways. She stumbles wildly backward, her boots scrambling for purchase. She fails to find traction on the slick, snowdusted stone, sending her crashing backwards toward the edge of the clearing.

A raw, jagged scream tears from Jules's throat, ripping through the thin, brittle atmosphere as she dives into the snowpack. She tackles the girl directly into the hard slate. Jules's knees pin her shoulders to the freezing dirt. Her hands grab desperately at the collar of the coat, violently shaking the child beneath her.

"Don't you kill him!" Jules shrieks, her voice breaking into a terrified roar as she glares down through her fogged glasses. "Don't you fucking touch him!"

As Jules tackles her violently into the freezing snowpack, Cadence's entire taur-like lower half curls tightly inward. She throws her fragile torso sharply to the side, absorbing the concussive impact of the icy slate against her own ribs to shield her hands. Her small, pale fingers clasp securely against her heaving chest, curling inward to protect the glass chamber of the metallic syringe from shattering beneath Jules's knee.

Jules's frantic screaming dies in her throat. The jagged roar echoes once more off the grey stone and vanishes into the falling powder.

She stops shaking the collar. Her grip loosens against the coat. She stares down through her tear-streaked glasses.

She's not fighting.

The girl is curled into a tight, shivering ball in the dirt, a fresh line of dark, hot blood dripping steadily from her split lip to stain the pristine white snow beneath her cheek.

Cadence looks up at the tall woman. Her pupils are wide and desperate.

She lies still beneath Jules's weight, her chest hitching softly as she extends her small, trembling hand upward. She holds out the unbroken syringe toward the cloudy glasses.

Jules's jaw goes completely slack as she stares down through the falling snow at the bleeding child. Jules's expression collapses. She rolls off the small, shivering frame, her knees hitting the icy slate beside her.

She buries her tear-streaked face deep into her own shaking palms, her shoulders heaving as she weeps softly into the freezing dust.

Ery kneels beside her, wings draping forward to shield Jules from the crosswind. Ery gently reaches out with her left hand, pressing her fingers warmly against Jules's shaking shoulder.

Jules flinches sharply at the sudden contact, physically recoiling. She slowly lifts her head from her hands, her cloudy glasses catching the soft, amber eyes of the moth-girl. Unable to maintain eye contact, Jules ducks her chin back into her coat.

Cadence clumsily pushes her four boots off the snowpack. She drags the back of her oversized, faded sleeve across her mouth, wiping the fresh, dark blood from her split lip.

She drops to her knees beside Minty, her hands trembling slightly in the thin air before aligning the sharp, metallic needle against the pulse point of Koa's feverish neck. Her thumb depresses the plunger, forcing the iridescent crimson stimulant directly into his bloodstream.

Koa's chest hitches with a sudden, violent gasp. His back arches rigidly against the stone.

His eyes flutter rapidly, snapping open as the potent drug rips his nervous system out of the coma.

Dragging a wet breath of the razor-sharp air into his lungs, his gaze darts frantically from the falling snowflakes to Minty's tear-streaked face.

He tries to push his uninjured shoulder off the frozen slate, but the muscles completely fail to fire. His head lolls limply back against the snowpack with a weak, wet wheeze, his body remaining humiliatingly heavy.

The empty cylinder drops from Cadence's pale fingers. It clatters loudly against the frozen stone.

Her four boots slowly shuffle backwards across the powder, gradually retreating to the perimeter of the clearing.

CHAPTER

13

NON-ESSENTIALS ABANDONED

A low, ionising roar vibrates through the monolithic stone, swallowed by a sudden, white-out storm that sweeps across the inclines.

The snowfall is thick, carrying a sharp, sulphurous scent that stings the back of the throat. The wind is a wall of pressurized air that rattles teeth against bone and turns the outworlders' exposed skin into a waxy, translucent white.

Jules leads the stumble through the white-out, her breath coming in shallow. She keeps one hand clamped over her mouth to filter the grit, her eyes squinting behind lenses clouded by a thick rime of frozen condensation. The world is reduced to the immediate six inches of grey stone before her boots.

Beside her, Ery's antennae are plastered flat against the curve of her skull, twitching violently as they pick up the erratic ambience of the storm. Every few steps, she stumbles, her boots sliding on the chemical slush forming over the permafrost.

A loading dock materializes through the turbulent grey as a monolithic slab of concrete. Its face is crisscrossed with deep, jagged fissures from centuries of shifting tectonic plates, the concrete scarred and pitted. The hangar door hangs partially open as a reprieve from the storm.

Jules wipes the stuck snow obscuring her vision as she looks up at the structure. "Up ahead! There's shelter!"

The group breaks into a staggering run. Jules and Minty each shoulder the last two single survival duffels, the weight shifting awkwardly as they scramble. Koa's boots drag uselessly through the sulphur-stained powder, his chin resting against his chest. Minty bears the brunt of his weight, her upper body hunched as she hooks an arm under his shoulder. Her heavy hooves punch deep craters into the frozen permafrost.

As Jules's boot strikes the metal threshold of the dock, a hidden bank of proximity sensors flickers with a dull, rhythmic red light. A piercing, mechanical shriek tears through the roar of the wind. Inside the ceiling, ancient hydraulics groan, shedding flakes of rust and frozen grease as the hangar door begins to descend.

"Move! Get him inside!" Jules's voice cracks, her voice nearly snatched away by the gale.

She grabs Ery by the shoulder of her cardigan and shoves her through the narrowing gap. Jules pivots back, her fingers locking into the collar of Koa's thermal coat to help Minty heave his limp frame over the rusted tracks of the door. The shadow of the descending iron slab looms over them.

Jules's head snaps back toward the blizzard.

Cadence is a hunched shape nearly swallowed by the grey, her wings dragging like broken sails through the slush. Jules lunges back into the teeth of the wind, her fingers clawing into the sleeve of her coat. She yanks the girl toward the dock.

They hit the threshold together. Cadence's boots clatter against the metal rail as she gallops forward, ducking her head to clear the descending iron. She disappears into the interior. Jules follows, but her boot catches a raised bolt on the uneven track. Her balance shatters, her shoulder slams into the freezing edge of the door, the impact ringing through her collarbone. She scrambles, palms sliding on the slick floor, but the door is lowering to the concrete.

Minty pivots her lower body, her four hooves skidding across the grit before locking into the rusted grooves of the floor. She throws her back against the moving steel slab and braces her forelegs against the stationary frame. Her spine bows into a rigid arch as she weaponizes her mass against the machine. The shriek of the hydraulics turns into a bone-deep grind.

"Jules, get up!"

Minty's voice is a guttural, wet strain. Her face is flushed a deep, frantic crimson. Her tail lashes behind her, striking the interior concrete wall in a desperate beat.

Jules rolls through the gap, the downdraft of the closing door whipping her hair across her eyes.

Minty recoils. She throws her weight backwards into the dark. The door slams shut with a final thud that vibrates through the soles of their boots and into their marrow.

The dark smells of stagnant oil.

Jules fumbles with the clip on her belt, her fingers numb and clumsy. She clicks her flashlight on, but the beam is a stuttering thread of light that dies almost as soon as it touches the cavernous ceiling.

"Damn it," Jules hisses, her voice echoing off the unseen girders above. She drops to her knees and digs into her grit-covered survival duffel, her hands shaking as she rummages through the collection of flat tools and resources.

The weak beam of the flashlight flickers one last time, illuminating a sprawl of industrial wreckage: massive, rusted crates stacked like tombstones.

Koa collapses onto the freezing concrete with a wet thud. His chest violently rattles. Under the dim, red pulse of a distant emergency light, his skin looks like curdled milk. The necrotic spore burn on his left arm has darkened, a black, pulsing web of veins crawling toward his elbow.

Ten feet away, Cadence sits against a stack of buckled metal crates. Her oversized researcher's coat is shredded at the hem, the white fabric stained grey by the caustic snowfall. A dark smear of dried blood crusts her split lip, eyes fixed on the floor in a vacant, glazed stare.

Cadence's boots gently thump against the floor as she forces herself to stand. They slide slightly on the oily ground, her lower half trembling with a caloric exhaustion. "Perimeter," she mutters, her voice a hollow rasp. "I have to... I have to check the rear exhaust vents."

She attempts to shuffle past Koa's prone form, her eyes avoiding the group. As her boots pass his shoulder, Koa's hand darts out. His fingers lock around her thin wrist. The movement is a desperate twitch of muscle, but his grip holds.

Cadence freezes. She stares down at the human hand on her arm, her pupils contracting into pinpricks.

She doesn't pull away.

Koa's eyes remain closed, his face twisted in strain, but he anchors himself to her with intensity. After an agonising minute, Cadence's shoulders slump, her wings loosening. She sinks back down to the concrete beside him, her tail curling protectively, if stiffly, around her own feet as she stares into the dark.

Jules moves toward a recessed alcove in the concrete wall, boots crunching over a layer of dried grit. Her hand sweeps across the bulkhead, searching for a physical latch or a rusted panel, but her palm brushes a smooth, cold pane of reinforced glass.

A machine blinks to life.

A high-pitched, harmonic whine rings through the hangar as the terminal draws power from a source that should have died centuries ago. Jules recoils, her heart slamming against her ribs, her hands flying up to protect her face.

The light isn't the guttering orange of a fire or the weak yellow of a dying flashlight; it is a piercing, surgical emerald.

Jules stands frozen, her shadow cast long and sharp. Her

breath hitches as she stares at the UI. It's crisp, the icons hovering with a ghostly, digital stability. Her fingers tremble as she reaches out, hovering over the sensor pad.

She slowly navigates the tree of files, her eyes wide behind her glasses. The screen scrolls through technical schematics of ventilation grids and hydraulic pressure logs until she lands on a high-priority document at the bottom of the directory.

```
EVACUATION MANIFEST - S4
```

The list is a cold, mathematical ledger of abandonment. Jules's eyes track the flickering text. It begins with heavy machinery.

```
Broken Power Converters (4)
Archaic Data Servers (12)
Hydraulic Press Dampeners (8).
```

She reaches a bolded header.

```
EXCESS WEIGHT / NON-ESSENTIALS ABANDONED.
```

Below the header, the list shifts to personal effects and low-priority assets. Boxes of hard-copy research. Decommissioned drones. Jules's finger hovers over the scroll key, her pulse thrumming visibly in the hollow of her throat.

At the very bottom of the ledger, a single line stands out in the glowing green text:

Biological Archive Subject: 92 (1).

Jules's hands drop from the terminal, her fingers curling into trembling claws at her sides. Her pupils dilate until the green light of the monitor fills her entire field of vision, reflecting off her lenses. She clicks on the entry, the screen updating to fill with logs.

LIST_ID: "Biological Archive Subject: 92"
ASSET_ID: BIO_ARCHIVE_92
CLASSIFICATION: NON-VIABLE / HIGH-MAINTENANCE
MANDATE: TERMINATION_VIA_EUTHANASIA
- **CO**: 902-B - SENIOR_RESEARCHER_ARIS

ID: SR_ARIS
TIMESTAMP: 11048.03.36
STATUS: VERIFIED_DEATH / BIOMASS_DISPOSED

"The chemical arrest was not performed. That brown fluid makes me feel fucking sick. System updated manually to report termination. She has been transferred to Stasis Vault 4. If you wake up, I am so sorry. I want you to sleep until the world is different, or until the power finally dies. I left you my coat so you wouldn't be cold if you woke up."

"If you wake up, I am so sorry."

She shivers, breath stuck in her throat. She can't speak. She can't scream.

The click of hooves and the soft rustle of a cardigan draw closer, pulled by the hypnotic green glow. They step into the light. Ery scans the screen. Her hand moves to her mouth.

Minty leans over Jules's shoulder, her ears twitching toward the glare. She reads the name at the bottom of the manifest.

"Aris," Minty whispers. "That's the name... on the collar. The one that's scribbled out on her coat."

The three women turn slowly. Their gazes drift from the terminal to the dark corner of the loading dock.

There sits Cadence.

She is huddled in the shadows beside Koa, her small frame looking woefully fragile against the rusted backdrop of the Axiom crates.

She is hunched over, her fingers moving with a focused diligence as she picks a stray, white thread off the sleeve of her oversized researcher's coat.

The coat Aris left her.

CHAPTER

14

You Fucking Idiot

The peaks are a vertical desert of silver and grey, a monochromatic expanse where the atmosphere thins into a void.

Every inhale is a shallow, frantic theft of oxygen that leaves the outworlders' chests burning with the sensation of swallowing needles. The wind is a continuous scream, that strips the heat from their marrow before it can settle against their skin.

Ery tramps through a single step behind Cadence, an arm outstretched before her face to fight back against the violent gale. She watches the back of the demi-human's head, tracking the rhythmic, mechanical bob of Cadence's shoulders. Cadence marches in an eerie silence, her four heavy boots finding purchase on the slick slate.

Ery lifts her chin, squinting toward the invisible horizon. There is no line where the stone ends and the sky begins. She pivots her upper body, her wings shivering under the fabric of her coat, to look back at the trail they have carved through the permafrost.

Not far behind, Jules and Minty are bent nearly double, their duffels strapped over their shoulders beside the sled's pull. Jules is a silhouette of desperate effort, her climbing harness humming with tension as her sneakers skid and slide on the glazed ice. Minty provides the bulk of the torque; each hoof-strike grinding into the stone with a hard thud. Between them, the litter lurches and bounces, holding a dead weight wrapped in thermal blankets, carrying the silent Koa deeper into the frostline.

His face is desaturated, his lips cracked and weeping a clear fluid that freezes into rime before it can drip. He is submerged in a hypoxic sleep, his head lolling with every lurch of the sled, his breath coming in shallow gasps that barely fog the air.

A sharp lurch over a jagged spine of slate jars the sled runners. The shock travels through the frame and into Koa's spine, snapping him into a state of delirious lucidity. His eyes fly open, the pupils darting as they struggle to focus through the white-out.

Jules's shoulders are vibrating with a deep, systemic exhaustion, her neck corded with tension as she leans into the harness. Minty's lower half struggling muscle, her hind legs buckling and catching with every stride under the crushing strain of his mass.

He watches a single bead of sweat roll down Jules's temple and freeze instantly against the crusted collar of her coat. He tracks the way Ery's wings shiver, not from the wind, but from the sheer effort of keeping her pace.

They are freezing to death.

Koa's fingers are dead wood as they fumble with the hefty steel carabiner at his chest. The metal is so cold it welds to the damp skin of his thumb. When he shoves at the gate, the skin tears away. He only feels the phantom weight of the line, the tension of the harness that connects his useless mass to Jules's trembling spine. With a wheezing gasp, he jams the gate open.

The sudden release of tension sends the harness whipping forward like a snapped bowstring.

Koa heaves his upper body to the side, rolling off the litter. His frame hits the deep, powdery snowbank with a muffled *thud,* his momentum carrying him toward the edge of the precipice.

Jules is jerked forward into the slush as the resistance vanishes. Her momentum turns against her. She slams into the glazed ice, her knees hitting the stone with a brittle crack. She spins around on her hands and knees, her breath wheezing in panicked bursts. Seeing Koa's dark shape sliding toward the precipice, she acts with frantic speed. She rips the clips of her duffel free first, letting the heavy bag land in the snow, before her fingers claw at the harness release. Lungs burning, she finally rips free of the sled tether. She lunges into the snowbank, her cargo trousers instantly soaking through with the biting cold as she scrambles down the slope after him.

"Koa!"

The scream is a raw thing that the gale tries to snatch away. She sees the dark, thrashing shape of him disappearing into the deep drift. Her fingers, slick with frozen sweat, claw at her own harness clips. She fumbles the release, lungs burning as she finally rips free of the tether. She lunges into the snowbank, her cargo trousers instantly soaking through with the biting cold as she scrambles down the slope after him.

She reaches him ten feet down the slope, her boots skidding through the powder until she collapses onto her knees beside him. Koa is hunched on all fours, his frame racked by a wet, hollow cough that spatters the snow with dark, oxygen-starved blood. It looks like black ink against paper. He tries to crawl further away, his movements uncoordinated, his hands clawing desperately at the ground.

"Koa! Stop! Get back on the sled!" Jules lunges for him, her fingers locking into the nylon straps of his harness with desperation. She tries to haul his weight upward, her injured knee shaking as she forces her weight on it. Koa's face is a mask of delirious terror, his eyes blown wide and glassy.

He punches Jules in the chest.

"Koa... what..." Jules's voice is a breathy wheeze, her lungs struggling to find air in the thin, biting atmosphere.

Koa doesn't answer with words. Instead, he lunges forward, his numb, blue fingers clawing at her shoulders. He shoves. It is a desperate, jerky heave.

"Jules, look at you!" Koa shrieks, the sound thin and reedy

as it's shredded by the wind. "You're going to fucking die! Let me go!"

Jules's boots skid on a patch of glazed slate beneath the powder. She stumbles back, her arms windmilling for balance as she hits the ice. He immediately turns, dragging his heavy, unresponsive lower body through the deep drift, clawing his way deeper into the edge of the precipice.

She launches herself from the ice, a desperate, lunging tackle that carries her through the air and onto his back. They crash into the snowbank together, the impact forcing a spray of powder into the air. Jules drives him down, using her weight to shove his face into the cold until his shoulders hit the underlying stone.

She pins his arms down against his chest, her knees locking over his hips to anchor him.

They are both sobbing.

Tears leak from the corners of their eyes only to freeze into jagged salt-trails on their waxy skin. Jules's glasses have vanished in the struggle; her world is a blurred, terrifying mess of grey and white as she screams into his face.

"Stop fighting me! You fucking idiot, stop fighting me!"

The fight drains out of Koa all at once, his muscles turning to water beneath her. He shatters into an ugly sob that shakes his entire frame. He goes limp in the snow, his head falling back as he stares up at the suffocated sky with unseeing eyes.

Minty and Ery loom out of the white-out, their frames hunched against the gale. Minty hooks her hands under Koa's armpits and heaves him upward, dragging him back toward the sled.

Blue tinted shadows are splayed across the walls of the icy cave.

The air inside is stagnant, smelling of old frost and recycled air. Outside, the storm remains a muffled, predatory roar, but inside, the only sound is the hiss of an Axiom oxygen canister.

Koa is propped up against Minty's duffel, his frame swallowed by the group's only thermal blanket. The silver fabric crinkles with every shallow, breath he takes. The plastic mask over his face fogs and clears in a steady, ghostly cycle, the elastic strap biting into the skin of his cheeks.

Ery and Minty are silent, overlapping heaps in the deeper gloom, their breathing synchronized by total exhaustion. Ery's wings are wrapped tightly around her like a shroud. Minty's tauric lower half is folded beneath her, her heavy hooves tucked close to her body to preserve the last of her warmth.

At the mouth of the cave, Cadence sits as a motionless silhouette. She remains upright on her four boots, her wing occasionally fluttering in response to the currents of air. She watches the snow spiral and catch against the rocky lip of the entrance.

Koa watches Jules from behind the fogged plastic of his mask.

She sits across the small chemical fire,

the pale orange light carving deep, exhausted lines into her face. Her eyes are sunken, framed by the dark, bruised violet of sleep deprivation. Her glasses are back on her face, though the wire frames are bent into a jagged, uneven slant that forces her to tilt her head to see through the centre of the lenses. The left glass is a spiderweb of hairline fractures, a mosaic of silver cracks that catches the firelight and shatters her vision into jagged orange slivers.

She has her boots off, her fingers methodically rubbing the bloodless flesh of her numbed toes. Her jaw is set in a hard line, the muscle thrumming at her temple as she tries to coax life back into her own frozen limbs.

"You should have... you should have done it."

Koa whispers, the words rattling against the plastic rim of the oxygen mask. His bloodshot eyes are wide, fixed on the flickering orange of the chemical fire. "I'm dragging the line. I'm dragging you all into the snow."

A raw, jagged sob hitches in his chest, making the silver thermal blanket crinkle sharply.

"I thought... once I couldn't carry the bags... you'd see. You'd see I'm just a drain." He reaches out a trembling, hand from beneath the silver foil, his fingers clawing at the air toward her. "Please. Don't let me be the reason you don't get home."

Jules freezes. The silence in the cave settles over the fire. She looks at him, her face sunken. She looks a decade older, her eyes dark pits of exhaustion.

"What do you think this is about?" She stares at him with a weary clarity. She points a red-raw finger toward the deeper gloom where Minty and Ery lie tangled together in sleep. "Look at them. You think Minty nearly burst her heart hauling that sled because you're a good pack-mule? You think Ery stayed a step behind Cadence all day to watch for a 'useful asset'?"

She leans forward, her shadow stretching long and jagged across the ice wall. "They hauled you because you're family, Koa. If you can't see that, then you're the only person in this cave who thinks you're useless. The leader board doesn't exist."

The shadows at the edge of the firelight shift as Cadence emerges. Her presence is heralded only by the soft thumps of her boots on the frosted stone. Her wings are folded so tightly against her spine they look like a jagged carapace of bone and hide beneath the tattered fabric of her coat.

She stops where the orange light meets the dark, her eyes darting between Koa's trembling frame and Jules's tired posture.

"He is currently excess weight," she drones. "His output is zero. To keep him in the line is to... to unbalance the equation."

She stands perfectly still, her pupils contracting into pinpricks.

Jules doesn't blink. Her jaw remains set, her gaze locking onto Cadence with a fierce intensity that makes the demi-human flinch. The orange light flickers in Jules's eyes.

"He isn't a variable, Cadence," Jules says, her voice low and serrated. "He's my brother. Now sit down and get warm, or you can go back to the corner of the cave you came from."

Cadence's head tilts sharply to the side.

She looks at the shivering, huddled forms of the outworlders and then back to Jules's defiant face.

She begins to move toward Koa, her tail dragging across the frozen stone with a sibilant hiss.

Slowly, awkwardly, she sinks to the stone beside Koa. Her four boots thump against the frosted floor as her legs fold beneath her. She leans the bulk of her sturdy, tauric side against him. Her gold and purple eyes remain fixed on the flickering chemical fire, her expression weary.

Koa looks at her from behind the fogged plastic of his mask, his breathing hitching once before it settles into a steadier rhythm. His head slowly falls back against the jagged rock, his hand reaching out to tentatively touch the frayed, stained edge of Cadence's sleeve.

Jules watches the hyper-lethal experiment and the broken pack-mule huddled together in the blue-tinted dark. A soft smile touches her lips, the first warmth to reach her eyes in days. She stands with a grimace; her injured knee locking and moves with a heavy limp toward them.

She gathers the edges of the thermal blanket, the silver foil shimmering in the firelight, and drapes it around them both, tucking the edges beneath Cadence's body and over Koa's shoulders. As Jules sits down on Cadence's other side, the demi-human flinches. Her muscles coil, her wings twitching.

But everything is still.

Cadence's eyes track Jules's profile with a wide stare. She watches her lean her head back against the ice wall and close her eyes, exhaling a long cloud of vapor. Cadence's breathing begins to lengthen. Her tail, lashed tight against her hind legs, goes slack, sliding across the frosted stone.

Cadence's shoulder sags, her weight shifting until it rests fully against Jules's side.

Her eyelids slip shut. Her fingers reach out, fumbling blindly until they lock onto the hem of Jules's cargo jacket, clutching the fabric gently. The mechanical alarm in her mind finally powers down, leaving her chest to rise and fall in the rhythmic drag of a dreamless sleep.

Jules stays awake for hours.

She rests her chin quietly on the girl's head, staring into the dark.

CHAPTER

15

I Can Do Better

There is no horizon, no stone, and no sky.

A blizzard is a total erasure of the world. High-altitude ice particles, fine as powdered glass, saturate the air.

Jules reaches into the side pocket of her survival duffel; her fingers numb and clumsy as they find the compass. The needle spins in erratic circles, driven mad by the ionising atmosphere of the peaks. She tries to blink away the vertigo, but the world has lost its floor and its ceiling.

The fractured left lens of her glasses splinters the grey into a thousand jagged shards. The mosaic of silver cracks turns the blizzard into a shifting, grey puddle of static that dances across her vision.

She tries to count her paces, to calculate a heading based on their last known waypoint, but the numbers dissolve into a high-pitched, internal whine.

Her knees buckle, her boots skidding on a patch of invisible ice. She stands paralysed, her heart thrashing against her ribs. Her lungs burn as she swallows the powdered glass of the air.

Ery steps forward. Her spine straightens as she moves to the front of the line. Her feathery antennae flare outward into the blinding landscape. To Jules, she has travelled in a random direction.

Jules lunges forward, her hand clawing into the wool of Ery's shoulder. Her voice is a terrified, freezing rasp that shears through the roar of the gale.

"Ery, stop! We're blind! Where are you even moving toward?"

Ery does not turn around. Her antennae twitching in sharp, precise zig-zags. "I don't know where the path is," she shouts back, her voice strained. "But the air is thick on the left, it's piling up against something solid. And on the right... there's nothing. That's the cliff."

Jules's grip on Ery's shoulder loosens.

She releases her shoulder and wraps her arms tightly around the girl's waist, burying her face between the base of Ery's wings to escape the biting grit. Behind her, Koa clings to the straps of Jules's pack, his chin resting against her shoulder. The three of them form a single, shivering line, with Minty's form moving close behind them, her hooves punching deep into the drifts.

At the rear of the line, Cadence's four-point gait begins to stutter. Her rear hooves drag through the powder,

leaving messy, shallow furrows. Her eyes are glazed, pupils dilating and contracting in a frantic pulse.

The snowstorm begins to quiet.

It begins to hum.

Cadence pauses upon her boot hitting a thin metallic plate welded to the ground.

That must be the ventilation system.

It smells like… ethanol.

Cadence's boots thump against polished linoleum that echoes off unseen walls.

Ten paces ahead, a figure stands in the glare. She is tall and clinical, her posture a rigid line of professional distance. A white lab coat billows behind her with every brisk step, catching the fluorescent light.

Her focus remains fixed on the glowing screen of a digital tablet in her hand, her thumb swiping through columns of scrolling data with an indifferent flick. Her heels strike the floor with a measured cadence that the girl can barely match.

As the figure marches, items begin to shed from her presence. A jagged wing-splint strikes the floor with a sharp ring before sliding into the fog. A glass blood vial, the crimson contents dark and thick, shatters against the tile.

Cadence lunges for them. Her front hooves skid on the polished linoleum, her rear boots scrambling for purchase as her centre of gravity collapses. She sweeps the items toward her chest, her wings twitching with a frantic hunger. "I can carry it," she whispers. Her voice is an echo in the sterile hall, small and tinny. "I am still within the margin. I can carry."

No matter how many steps Cadence forces into her trembling legs, the distance to the lab coat widens. The figure is a retreating sail. The faster Cadence scrambles, the further the ghost recedes, drifting into the absolute white at the end of the corridor.

Cadence's front boots skid out from under her, and she slams into the icy ground, her chin striking the frozen linoleum with a crack. She lunges forward from the ground, her hands scraping frantically at the air, trying to snag the hem of a coat far out of reach.

"Wait," she whispers. "I can do better. Please. Slow down." Cadence is reduced to a small, four-legged shape shivering in the drifts, her shoulders heaving.

Minty pivots her frame with a skidding lurch, her obsidian-hard hooves punching deep into the permafrost. The frantic whispering catches in the fine fur of her ears through the ionising roar of the gale.

She looks back through the churning void and sees Cadence has veered ten feet into the blinding white, her wings dragging through the drifts like broken sails. She is on her knees, crawling, her hands clawing at the empty air.

Minty's large ears pin back flush against her skull. She sees the vacancy in the guide's eyes.

Cadence is a ghost chasing a ghost.

"Everyone! Stop! She's losing it!" Minty's voice cracks against the wind, the scream raw and jagged. She turns and moves backward into the drifts, her forelegs slamming into the snow. She plants her weight, her spine arching as she shields Cadence's trembling frame from the direct assault of the wind. The snow sprays against Minty's coat, but in the lee of her body, the air settles.

The sudden slack in the line sends Jules and Koa stumbling. The group turns as one, the tether of their shared struggle pulling them back into the heart of the whiteout.

Cadence has collapsed into a foetal position beneath Minty's shadow. She is a small, four-legged knot of fabric and shivering limbs, her forehead pressing hard into the frozen slush. Her shoulders heave with a rhythmic, broken shudder as she sobs into the ice.

Jules, Koa, and Ery crumble into the deep powder, their bodies overlapping as they drop into a tight huddle around Cadence's prone form. Ery's wings flare one last time before wrapping inward, the membranes smothering the group. She creates a dark, humid pocket of shared warmth.

Jules pulls Cadence's head against her chest, her frozen fingers fumbling to find the pulse at the girl's neck. Her skin brushes the thick, scarred hide of Cadence's throat, feeling the desperate thrum of her heart.

"Ery, thank you. Just keep them down a little longer," Jules whispers, her raspy voice shearing through the humidity.

Her eyes pivot to Koa, barely awake. "Koa... hey, look at me. Stay awake, okay?" She traces the bruised topography of his face with a numb thumb. "Your lips... they're so blue. Indigo."

Koa's chest rattles against the fluid rising in his lungs. "It's so cold…" he wheezes. The dark, obsidian web of the spore burn on his arm pulses against his frayed coat, the charred veins throbbing with an erratic rhythm.

Jules presses a thumb into her own fingers, staring at the skin through her cracked lens. "White," she breathes, her voice trembling. She swallows hard.

She turns her gaze toward Minty. The taur's muscles are jumping beneath her wool coat in spasms that shake her body. Jules reaches out, resting a hand on Minty's shivering flank.

"I can't," Minty gasps, her teeth chattering so hard they click like stones. "I'm trying, Jules, I'm trying to hold still."

"I know. You're doing the best you can," Jules murmurs.

Cadence's eyes begin to clear as the collective body heat of the group grounds her. She looks up, her soft eyes finding Jules's sunken face through the gloom.

It smells like… rain.

The outworlders crest the lip of the plateau with a collective stumble, their boots punching deep craters into an unbroken blanket of snow. The world here is muffled, the atmosphere suspended in a weightless, gentle fog that turns the landscape into a white desert of softened edges. Above them, the sky is a soft, glowing expanse of bruised indigo, the stars reduced to distant, smudged embers behind the veil of the mist. Looming through the stillness is the Axiom facility, a brutalist monolith of concrete that pierces the sky.

The moment the monolith enters Cadence's field of vision, her four boots lock into the hidden slate beneath the snow. Her eyes are fixed on the facility's primary exhaust port, reflecting the monolithic grey of the building.

The outworlders stumble toward the jagged, rusted maw of a toppled cooling tower. They move into the shadow of the iron cavern, the air inside turning stagnant and tasting of flaking rust.

Jules sinks to her knees, the metal floor groaning beneath her. She pulls her survival duffel into her lap, while Minty sits exhausted beside her, clutching the group's only other remaining bag filled with nothing but hefty tools. Jules's bag is dangerously light. She sweeps her hand across the interior, her nails catching on the seams.

She pulls out four rectangular, foil-wrapped bricks. They are the colour of wet slate, stamped with the Axiom's geometric logo. From the very bottom of the bag, she unearths the last two bottles of filtered water, the plastic crinkling under her touch. She stares at them for a long moment. She pinches the edge of the first sachet, the foil resisting her stiff, bloodless fingers before it tears with a sharp crinkle. She turns the canvas inside out to shake out the last of the grit before folding the depleted pack flat.

The scent of cardboard and stale minerals fills the immediate air. She hands a piece and a shared bottle of water to Koa's blue-tinged fingers. She repeats the process for Minty and Ery, passing the second bottle between them. Jules breaks her own block in half. The sound is a dry, hollow snap that echoes up the curved walls of the tower. Putting half back in the packet, she takes her own half-brick and bites into it, the dry substance sticking to the roof of her mouth.

Jules shifts her weight, looking through a jagged tear in the tower's side, her eyes finding the dark, four-legged notch against the white horizon. Cadence stands at the lip of the plateau, a small silhouette carved against the indigo sky. From this distance, Jules can see the tension in the girl's frame.

She looks at the facility beyond her, the heart of every horror they've uncovered.

"Those fucking monsters," Jules hisses under her teeth, her voice snarling. She stares into the orange embers of the chemical fire, her fingers locking around her pen. "And we thought testing on animals was the bottom. This... this is evil. Systemic evil."

"She was a monster, too," Her voice rises into a raw, serrated edge. "To leave Cadence for dead just so she could catch her flight on time. Aris was a fucking coward."

Click.

Before Jules can finish her breath, Cadence is inside the circle of the firelight. Her posture is locked rigid. In her hand, she grips her glaive, with the primary blade levelled inches from Jules's throat.

"Retract the statement," Cadence drones. Her voice is hollow. Her eyes are fixed on Jules's face, unblinking.

"Senior Researcher Aris was the architect of the evacuation. Her decisions were governed by the Axiom Directive. I was a non-viable unit. Discarding non-essential assets to preserve the fleet's survival margin is... it is the highest form of discipline."

Jules doesn't flinch. She sneers. "Discipline? Is that what you call it? She reported you as *disposed biomass*. She told the company you were dead to avoid an audit."

Cadence's claws scrape against the rusted wall of the tower. Her pupils contract into sharp dots, the irises flickering. "Biological forms are volatile," she insists, her voice tight. "She ensured the security of the fleet. She followed the logistics. She was... she was a perfect scientist."

"She was a coward," Jules counters. She leans forward, deliberately closing the gap until the cold steel nicks the skin of her neck. A single, thin bead of blood wells up, rolling slowly into the crusted collar of her coat. Jules winces at the sting but refuses to look away. "She looked at the people who told her to kill you, and she was too scared to say no. She put you in a box and hoped you would stay frozen forever because she was scared of a performance review."

"The Directive is absolute!" Cadence shrieks. The drone finally shatters, her voice breaking into a prepubescent crack. Her tail lashes violently behind her, striking the metal floor with a booming thud. "I was hardware!"

Jules looks past the shaking, shimmering steel at the scarred, shivering child behind it.

Her eyes soften. "She had a choice to be a mother or a researcher," Jules whispers.

“She didn't leave behind hardware, Cadence. She left *you*."

Cadence’s grip on the glaive convulses. The tremor travels from her fingers up her scarred arms, vibrating through her shoulder blades.

Cadence pivots her body, whipping the glaive away from Jules’s neck and hurling it across the cooling tower with a violent, uncoordinated surge of strength.

The carbon-steel blade shrieks as it strikes the curved metal wall. A spray of sparks showers the dark as dying stars, and the sharp *clang* of the impact echoes upward into the hollow of the tower. The glaive drops to the floor, the primary edge chipped and the reinforced shaft bent into a useless, mocking curve.

Cadence stands heaving, her chest rattling that fog the freezing air. Her tail is tucked tight between her hind legs. She turns, her wings hanging limp, dragging through the grime and soot as she leaves the vessel.

"Cadence."

The dragging sound of the wings stops. Cadence remains motionless in the shadows, her back turned to the firelight.

"Take the rest of the food," Jules says softly. She holds out the dry square of synthetic grey.

The high-frequency vibration in her wing-claws produces a faint, metallic hum against the tower wall.

Jules softly presses her thumb into the foil of the ration brick. "Cadence, take it. I'm not asking."

For a long minute, the only sound is the low-frequency hum of the mountain. Then, Cadence pivots, her four boots shuffling in the grime as she turns to face the firelight.

She steps back into the fringe of the glow. She reaches out, her scarred fingers trembling with a high-frequency vibration as they snatch the calories from Jules's palm. Without a word, she turns back toward the jagged exit of the tower and disappears into the indigo dark of the plateau, her wings dragging a fresh, deep trail through the snow.

The chemical fire has burned down to a dull, orange ember, casting a faint glow.

Jules, Minty and Koa are fitfully asleep, their frames heaps of thick coats and thermal blankets as they rest their heads against the edge of Koa's litter.

Ery stares through a jagged fissure in the iron wall, her gaze fixed on the monolithic spine of the facility in the distance. The silhouette is a dark spear against the bruising indigo of the star-choked sky.

The silence doesn't last very long.

The sound of a boot dragging through the snow reaches her ears. Ery's antennae pivot sharply toward the exit. The sound is erratic, and heading away from the group toward the sheer drop of the plateau's edge.

Ery finds her at the brink of the camp, a four-point silhouette carved from the starlight. Cadence is moving hastily, her wings tucked into her spine. Her boots skid on a patch of slick slate, and her breath comes in bursts that bloom around her head.

Ery steps down the steep, powder-heavy bank toward the retreating silhouette, her boots sinking deep into the snow. Mid-stride, her heel catches a hidden shelf of black ice buried beneath the drift. Her balance shifts, the weight of her damp cardigan pulling her sideways. She slides down the remainder of the slope before she comes to a rest in a soft spray of displaced snow.

Cadence freezes. She stops her retreat, pivoting her upper body to track the source of the sound. She remains motionless, her tracking the shivering shape of Ery as the moth-girl slowly pushes herself up from the drifts, shaking her wings free of snow.

Ery reaches her with a staggering gait, her breath wheezes. Her hand, raw and shivering, reaches out to find Cadence's small, cold palm.

The rigidity leaks from Cadence's frame. She draws a breath of silence inwards, sagging forward until her forehead comes to rest against the dirty, rough wool of Ery's cardigan. Her small chest vibrates against Ery's ribs.

Her fingers tighten with a desperate strength.

Cadence remains stiff for a long moment, her ears pressed flat against her skull and her tail tucked tight against her hind legs.

"Ery," she breathes. "I... I am afraid. I don't want to go back home."

CHAPTER 15

Bitter Snow

The atmosphere thickens into a pressurised tomb of stagnant air.

Thirty feet of reinforced lead and concrete loom overhead, a frozen, open maw that swallows the howling wind as the outworlders cross the threshold. The sudden, heavy transition into the stagnant stillness of the facility vibrates through their marrow.

The air tastes of old frost, recycled ozone, and the bitter scent of three-hundred-year-old cooling fluid. Jules wipes a hand across her mouth; her palm comes away stained with the copper-dark smear of burst lung capillaries. She looks down at the litter rattling behind Minty, where Koa lies slack, his skin faded to the colour of wet ash.

The weight of the litter ripples through Minty's shoulders and hooves. She lets out a low huff as the low heat of the facility begins to cook the frost off their coats.

The corridors are brutalist, seamless grey slabs that stretch into the dimming darkness. Narrow, reinforced skylight panels catch the bruised-purple of the evening, casting long, geometric shadows across the recessed workspaces. Bolted-down polymer desks and rows of hard, ergonomic seating. Everything is coated in a fine, grey shroud of undisturbed dust that Jules's sleeve catches as she brushes past, leaving a dark streak on the plastic.

The group passes behind thick panes of reinforced glass. Inside vats, suspended in browned, stagnant preservation fluid, are skeletons. Some with too many limbs, others with skulls fused into jagged, unfinished crowns, drift in the amber dark.

Ery presses her arm across her nose to stem the sudden drip of dark blood. She looks at the glass, her eyes reflecting the rows of corpses.

Cadence's coat swishes against her flanks, the fabric stained with soot and salt. Her gaze is fixed on the lines separating the panelling of the floor.

The corridor opens into a cavernous, vertical shaft. At its centre sits a massive, circular transfer platform. A disc of pitted industrial steel, thirty feet across. Four hefty, reinforced gates are spaced evenly around its circumference, marking different points of entry from the surrounding hallways.

Minty drags the litter onto the cold metal grate. At the centre of the disc stands a control plinth, topped with a rusted, multi-stage lever. Cadence approaches it.

Her hands, trembling, grip the cold iron. She throws her weight into the mechanism.

The gears beneath them grind as the platform lurches upwards. It rises through the hollow core, gathering speed with a hydraulic groan. As they ascend, the walls ignite with the scale of the Axiom's ledger. Murals of biological data flicker in emerald light; scrolling columns of genetic code rain down the concrete. Maps of the planet's "sectors" pulse in a bruised, rhythmic red.

Jules grips the vibrating rail, her cracked glasses catching the glare. Her gaze snags on a projection of the very path they had bled across for weeks. It is a schematic. She sees the culling points, the survival triggers, and the "Yield-Stress" zones.

They were never visitors.

They were just new, unmapped variables introduced into a three-hundred-year-old experiment.

Koa's body jolts on the litter, a wet, reedy cough tearing through his throat. A spray of fresh, dark blood spatters the silver foil of his thermal blanket as vivid crimson droplets. His glossy gaze catches the walls paned with the information of their insignificance.

They arrive at the facility's nadir, the lift locking into place with a shivering industrial thud. It smells like ethanol.

The chamber is a cavernous void of obsidian and reinforced glass. At its centre stands the monolithic pillar of black stone, surrounded by colossal, humming, interlocking rings. Magnetic distortion shimmers in the air.

The active core at the centre of the chamber produces a wet, oppressive heat that turned the atmosphere uncomfortably humid.

Minty and Ery strip off their thick thermal coats, piling the sodden heaps into a dark corner of the obsidian room alongside the last survival duffel. Beside them, Jules peels the heavy coat from Koa's frame.

Set into the mirror-black stone of the floor, directly beneath the shadow of the central pillar, is a massive, circular ring. A dormant eye of lead, copper, and reinforced glass. Jules and Minty heave the litter across the threshold. The scrape of the metal runners against the seamless floor echoes upwards into the dark.

Cadence moves toward an obsidian plinth topped with a recessed, industrial keyboard of matte-grey keys. Her fingers, trembling, hover over the board for a single heartbeat. She presses a leaden, recessed toggle at the base of the plinth.

A flicker of cold, light bleeds from the gaps between the keys, and then the monolithic arrays above surge to life.

A blur of system diagnostics cascades down the walls in a vertical rain of white text. The machine breathes, a sudden vent of pressurized, ice-cold air whistling from the floor grates. The screen stabilizes, the light shifting from a harsh white to an emerald. The text reflects in the gold and purple of Cadence's retinas.

```
[LOG_START: 1104.92.3]
SYS: KERNEL_LOADED... OK
SYS: NODE_SYNC_ESTABLISHED (FM-C3 / AXIOM_PRIME)
AUD: INITIATING HABITAT_METRICS_SCAN...

- OBJECTIVE: ACCELERATED_EVOLUTIONARY_STRESS_TEST
- ATMOS_02: 0.04%
```

```
- TOX_INDEX: 98.2%
- CURRENT_STATUS: HABITAT_VOID
```

A rotating wireframe of the planet pulses a stagnant, bruised red in the air above the plinth. Beneath the hologram, a final, cold calculation displays in a series of rapidly scrolling digits.

```
- PROJECT_FM: COMPLETED
- C/B: MARGINAL_LOSS_ON_BIOLOGICAL_RESOURCES
- ACTION: STRUCTURAL_ABANDONMENT_OF_FM
- MANDATE: SALVAGE_ASSETS
```

Jules watches the green light spill over the dark blood on Koa's blanket. She looks up and catches the text on the screen.

"Cadence..." Jules's voice scrapes, barely audible over the hum of the rings.

Cadence turns. Her eyes are wide.

"The experiment is over," Jules says. "Look at the screen. We're leftovers."

A thin, violet beam scythes through the chamber in a three-dimensional arc. It skips over Minty's tensed shoulders and Ery's drooping, mist-slick antennae, dismissing them as background noise. The light lingers only on Cadence, mapping the geometry of her retinas.

The arrays overhead reset with a sharp, electronic chirp.

```
SYS: INITIATING SUBJECT_SCAN_ROUTINE
```

```
[1]
- TARGET: U_92
- CLASS: VERIFIED_ASSET
- INTEGRITY: 14.02%
- MANDATE: ASSET_RETENTION_ENGAGED

[2]
- TARGET: [1] UNMAPPED_CARBON_UNIT
- CLASS: UNRECOGNISED_BIOMASS
- INTEGRITY: N/A
- MANDATE: NULL EXPIRATION_IMM_DETECTED

[3]
- TARGET: [2] UNMAPPED_CARBON_UNIT
- CLASS: UNRECOGNISED_BIOMASS
- INTEGRITY: N/A
- MANDATE: NULL EXPIRATION_IMM_DETECTED

[4]
- TARGET: [3] UNMAPPED_CARBON_UNIT
- CLASS: UNRECOGNISED_BIOMASS
- INTEGRITY: N/A
- MANDATE: NULL EXPIRATION_IMM_DETECTED

[5]
- TARGET: [4] UNMAPPED_CARBON_UNIT
- CLASS: UNRECOGNISED_BIOMASS
- INTEGRITY: N/A
- MANDATE: NULL EXPIRATION_IMM_DETECTED
```

Cadence's tail lashes against her legs, a sharp, whip-like motion that stirs the dust. She turns back to the console, her fingers hammering the matte-grey keys to force a diagnostic, trying to find a way to reclassify the dying people behind her.

The plinth emits a rhythmic, high-pitched error tone.

"Let me," Jules wheezes. She lunges for a secondary diagnostic panel, her movements clumsy and frantic.

The moment her finger grazes the edge of the port, the circuit completes. A violent arc of blue static snaps into Jules's knuckles. Her fingers lock in a rigid, clawed spasm around the metal. The kinetic kick of the shock hurls her backwards; her boots skid across the mirror-black obsidian, and her fractured glasses spin away, clattering into the dark. She hits the floor with a thud, her lungs seizing in a paralysed chest as the smell of scorched ozone rises from her skin.

A strong, red light beyond the terminal drowns the room in red.

```
SYS: EXTERNAL_INTERFERENCE_DETECTED
- SOURCE: [1] UNMAPPED_CARBON_UNIT → FM-C6
- ACTION: SECURITY_DISCHARGE_COMPLETE
- SYS: ELEVATE COMPROMISE_RISK_INCREASING
```

Cadence's gaze swings back to the screen. She yells back in a language of keystrokes, her small hands vibrating. The keyboard is unresponsive and unyielding.

```
SYS: ASSET_NEURO_SYNC_IRREGULAR
SYS: COERCION_FLAG_DETECTED
SYS: LOCKING_LOCAL_INPUTS
```

"No," Cadence whispers, the word lost in the sudden, heavy grind of the floor.

The aperture ring beneath the central pillar begins a counter-rotating slide. Lead and copper scream against reinforced glass. The ionizing charge in the air thickens. The scent of ozone becomes a physical sting on the back of the throat.

The arrays display a final, non-negotiable directive in towering blocks:

```
SYS: INITIATING_IMMEDIATE_ASSET_SALVAGE

- OBJ: SECURE_PROJECT_YIELD
- FM_DIM_DOOR_1: ROTATION_START... 13%...
- FM_DIM_DOOR_1: ROTATION_START... 29%...
```

Cadence looks away from the screen. She looks at the indigo of Koa's lips as he lies motionless on the litter. She looks at the wet crimson dripping from Ery's nose, the moth-woman's wings shivering in the magnetic draft. She looks at Minty, whose large ears are pinned flat against her skull as she cowers from the industrial shriek of the rings. Nearby, Jules picks her glasses up with a trembling hand, the fractured lenses refracting the red emergency light.

The machine is preparing to go home.

It just doesn't intend to take the family I found with it.

Cadence's gaze breaks from the terminal. She looks at Jules, still gasping on the obsidian floor.

There's no math that can fix this.

Cadence reaches into the shredded lining of her coat, her fingers fumbling to find the cold, silver cylinder. She rips it from her coat, the liquid swaying a sickly brown. Her hands vibrate with a high-frequency tremor that makes the glass chatter against her teeth as she pulls the vial into the clinical, red glare of the alarms.

Minty's pupils contract as she realises what the girl is holding. She lets out a low half-formed sob and her hooves skid as she lunges forward, her coat swishing. Ery's antennae twitch, her wings flaring as she stumbles toward the plinth.

Jules's eyes lock on the silver cylinder, and her heart pauses against her ribs. She desperately pushes herself off the ground. "Cadence don't-" her voice is a broken rasp, her lungs still seizing from the shock.

Cadence turns away to look at the ticking percentage one more time.

- FM_DIM_DOOR_1: ROTATION_START... 88%...

Before jamming the needle into the soft, scarred hide of her neck.

A sharp, guttural gasp escapes her. Her wings snap open in an involuntary spasm, the joints popping with the sound of dry wood. The force of the expansion scythes through the air, sending a spray of accumulated soot and mountain frost into the emerald glare of the arrays.

Cadence's four legs buckle, her boots skidding and clattering on the black stone as her motor functions unspool. Jules and Minty scramble to her side, their hands reaching for her. Cadence is already dead weight. She hits the floor hard, her chest heaving in shallow tremors. A thin, white foam flecks her lips.

The mechanical hum of the room shifts to a piercing, high-pitched scream of cooling fans and panicked processors as the screen sprays out lines of updated information.

```
SYS: ASSET_VALUATION_LOSS_DETECTED

- BIO: SYSTOLIC_COLLAPSE (UNIT_92)
- BIO: NEURAL_ARREST_IMMINENT

SYS: TRIAGE_PROTOCOL_A_ENGAGED

- FM_DIM_DOOR_1: FORCED_DIVERT
- FM_DIM_DOOR_1: NEW_DST
- FM_DIM_DOOR_1: ROTATION_START... 80%...
- FM_DIM_DOOR_1: ROTATION_START... 96%...
- FM_DIM_DOOR_1: STABLE
```

The aperture ring in the floor erupts in a deafening, pressurised roar. The vacuum roars between worlds. Through the unstable, shimmering indigo haze of the breach, there is the absolute, terrifying dark of a mountain night on the other side, carrying the sharp, scent of oxygen.

The pressure differential is a physical assault, a screaming gale that pulls at their clothes and stings their eyes. The dead air of the Axiom begins to bleed out into the void, and for the first time in weeks, the outworlders feel the dense, life-giving weight of Earth's atmosphere rushing in to meet them.

Lungs that had been weeping fluid and starving for weeks suddenly inflate with rich, oxygenated air. The copper taste in Jules's mouth is drowned by the sharp, cold scent of wet pine.

The outworlders freeze.

Koa rolls off the litter, his body fuelled by a frantic burst of adrenaline.

"Grab her! Get her to the door!" Koa's voice is a reedy, desperate shriek.

Despite his indigo lips and the necrotic web on his arm, he lunges forward. He, Minty, and Ery seize Cadence's dead weight by the arms, their fingers digging frantically into the fabric of her coat.

They begin to drag her toward the shimmering haze of the doorway. Her hooves scrape against the mirror-black stone, leaving jagged white tracks in the obsidian. Minty's muscles cord and strain, her face twisted in her physical defiance.

Jules stops.

She remains on her knees, the gale of the opening whipping her hair across her face. She watches as Cadence's skin boils along her ribs, dark blood welling and steaming where the violent rush of air touches it. She sees the way the girl's wing are curling into themselves, blackened and brittle.

She is a prisoner.

"Stop! Stop pulling her!"

Jules's voice cracks, a raw sound that tears through the roar of the vacuum. She lunges forward, tackling Minty's arm and forcing her to lose her grip.

"Jules, what are you doing?" Koa screams, his hands still clutching Cadence's coat. "We have to go!"

"We can't take her!" Jules points a trembling, waxy finger at the blood pooling under Cadence's wings, at the way the girl is literally disintegrating in the air they are breathing so greedily. "Look at her, Koa! It's killing her! The oxygen is burning her alive!"

Jules sinks to the floor, her hands hovering over Cadence. She gently places her palm on her degrading hand, holding it in hers.

"We can't keep her," Jules sobs, the sound fluttering into the gale.

Cadence lies on the black stone, her body a battlefield of competing toxins. She is choking on the cocktail of Fermata's rot and the rich, "clean" Earth air that pours through the aperture like liquid fire.

Through the haze of her failing vision, she sees the salt trails carving through the soot on Jules's cheeks and the way Minty's hand is still desperately buried in the fabric of her coat.

With a slow, agonising effort, Cadence reaches up. Her fingers, slick with the blood weeping from her blistered skin, wrap around Minty's wrist. She pushes her own weight out of Minty's grip, her hooves sliding back an inch on the obsidian.

She stares at them with a pair of exhausted eyes.

The pressure tugs at the outworlders, inviting them back into the dark of the mountain night.

Koa, his chest heaving as the rich,

thick oxygen of Earth pulls at his starving lungs, looks one last time at the shivering girl. He stumbles backwards, his boots sliding through the dark blood on the humid obsidian, until the haze swallows him whole, drawing him into the darkness.

Minty's hand lingers in the air, trembling, before she pulls it back to her own chest, clenching a fistful of her own heavy coat. She looks at the tracks her hooves left in the obsidian and steps over the threshold.

Jules looks at the way Cadence's chest hitches, at the blood leaking on the black stone, and she finally stands. Her legs are shaky, but steps backwards, her eyes never leaving Cadence's, until the indigo light catches her shoulders and draws her gently into the void.

Ery steps up the platform of the structure, standing at the very centre of the ring, her wings flapping wildly in the draft. She looks back at the solitary, bleeding shape of Cadence, huddled at the base of the obsidian pillar.

Ery reaches out. Her thin, trembling fingers wrap around the rusted lever bolted to the inner rim of the ring. It is a primitive piece of industrial hardware, caked in centuries of dust and oxidation. Through the shimmering heat and the violent distortion of the portal, Ery holds Cadence's gaze.

Ery throws her entire, fragile weight into the mechanism. She yells, the sound lost to the roar of the breach, as she heaves the iron handle downward.

The physical circuitry snaps with a bone-jarring industrial

crack.

A massive blast of force ripples through the obsidian floor, a discharge of light that arcs across the rings. The door snaps shut like a closing eye, the indigo dark of Earth vanishing in a microsecond. The connection is severed with a final, booming thud that shakes the very foundation of the mountain and throws Cadence's battered frame across the obsidian until she slams against the base of the central pillar.

One by one, the emerald monitors flicker and die, their light receding into the glass. Cadence is alone in the pitch-black vault, the only sound the laboured whistle of her own lungs.

It's cold. The machine has stopped moving.

Cadence's diaphragm releases a spasm that forces a slurry of bile and brown fluid from her throat. It spatters the black stone in a dark, steaming puddle. She lies there for a moment, her cheek pressed against the obsidian, her eyes tracking the way the liquid slowly beads on the non-porous surface.

A guttural, thin groan escapes her.

She reaches forward. Her fingers, slick with the fluid weeping from her blistered palms, find the hairline fracture between two obsidian floor tiles. She hooks her nails into the gap and pulls. The fabric of the oversized researcher's coat bunches around her chest, dragging across the floor with the sound of coarse sandpaper, thoroughly staining in her blood.

She hauls her weight forward inch by agonizing inch, her breath coming in a series of wet hitches that rattle in her ribcage.

The hallways are shrouded in lightless dark. She passes the row of reinforced glass vats.

Her gold and purple eyes catch the drifting skeletons suspended in the amber dark of stagnant fluid. They float in the silence as she scrapes past them, dragging her wreckage through a graveyard of drafts.

The deep antiseptic smell of ethanol and recycled ozone begins to thin. A sudden, biting draft of mountain air catches the hem of her coat.

Cadence reaches the intake threshold. She drags her body over the cold metal lip of the door and collapses into the snow.

It stings the blisters on her hands and melts instantly where it touches her weeping skin, turning into a thin, pink slush. She continues to crawl, her forearms ploughing furrows through the white until she is clear of the facility's shadow. Behind her, she draws a trail of dark warm blood across the powder.

She rolls onto her back. The movement is slow, her boots carving deep arcs in the snow before she settles. Her chest heaves, each inhalation a steady plume of vapour that rises and vanishes into the dark.

The thick, sulphurous fog of Fermata is slowly drifting apart. The high-altitude winds tear at the haze, shredding the clouds into thin wispy threads. The grey ceiling of the world thins, revealing the cold, crystalline depth of the universe.

Cadence stares.

Tens of thousands of stars puncture the indigo dark. Distant, warm pinpricks of white light.

The gold and purple of her eyes reflect the celestial mess.

Her tail lies motionless in the snow.

Her wings are tattered and still.

The mountain has stopped humming.

She closes her eyes.

It's quiet.

It's so quiet.

Epilogue

Chapters IV - V

CHAPTER

One Last Time

Jules's head snaps back.

A concussive swell of pressure turns the Swiss horizon into a spinning wheel of deep violet and orange.

She is on her knees, the powder of the Les Attelas overlook pressing into her palms. The nausea is a violent, churning knot in her gut, making the distant, twinkling lights of the ski village below blur into a chaotic mess of gold. She reaches out, her hand sweeping through the cold snow until her numb fingers strike a familiar curve of cold, thin metal.

Jules pulls her glasses from the drift. Her hands are shaking as she slides them onto the bridge of her nose. The left lens is a web of silver cracks, fracturing the alpine evening into a thousand jagged shards.

She must have dropped them. She must have hit the ground hard.

She sits back on her heels, gasping, waiting for the world to stop rotating.

She draws a long, shivering breath of the alpine air, but it feels too thin, too empty, as if she had resurfaced too fast.

She looks out at the distant peaks. The white snow and the gold, twinkling lights of Verbier are so steady in their luxury that they look like a painted backdrop.

Her gaze drops, sweeping over the campsite. The heavy, expensive luggage sits exactly where it was dropped, the dark leather untouched by the damp. Their battery-powered lantern sits on the pebbles, undisturbed.

Jules's numb fingers brush against the rigid, laminated edges of her itinerary. She pulls the corner of the paper out, staring at the dense, calculated blocks of text through her fractured lens.

We… need to get home. It's late.

The familiar, frantic urge to check the time stalls in her throat. She turns her head slowly, her gaze sweeping over the others.

Koa is seated on the cold pebbles near the edge of the drifts, his legs stretched out. His head is resting against the dark, expensive leather of a duffel bag, his eyes closed.

Minty stands at the far end of the ledge. Her head is held high against the biting alpine wind as she draws in a long, steady breath of the clean air.

Ery stands at the very brink of the overlook, her antennae gently swaying in the soft evening swell. Her silhouette is a sharp, quiet line against the darkening sky.

Jules looks back down at the laminated sheet in her hand. She pulls the thick, calculated blocks of text entirely from her pocket and holds the itinerary out into the crosswind. The plastic surface reflects the bruised violet of the evening.

The transit times, the equipment lists, the rigid geometry of her life.

She lets go.

The wind catches the papers lifting it for a second before a sudden downdraft snatches it away. Jules watches as the pages tumble uselessly over the edge of the Les Attelas ridge, vanishing into the vast, dark expanse of the valley below.

She walks across the pristine snow toward the edge of the overlook, her sneakers crunching softly in the powder.

Jules stops at the very edge of the world. The alpine air is a sharp, cold weight against her skin. She comes to a halt beside Ery, their shoulders brushing in the quiet evening.

Ery turns her head slowly. Her antennae are still.

She offers a soft, weak smile.

She leans forward, her hands grasping the wool of Ery's

sleeve as she pulls her into a long embrace. She buries her face into the crook of Ery's neck, the scent of almond milk and cold mountain air filling her lungs.

Jules feels the first hot tracks of tears carving through the rime of frost on her cheeks. They sting against the cold.

The feeling is the only thing she knows for certain.

CHAPTER

Three Hundred Years To Hit the Ground

Her vision is flooded from all angles by a blinding fog.

Cadence remains anchored to the wet earth, her compact frame rigid, an uncontrollable shudder rattling her spine. Her chest hitches in erratic gasps, desperately pulling at the tasteless vapor. Beneath her knees, the picnic blanket is reduced to a shredded nest of torn, wet threads. Her dirt-caked fingers are buried deep within the fray, hooked and tangled so tightly into the ruined wool that her knuckles bleed white from the strain. Her wide, heterochromatic eyes dart wildly across the fragments of the blanket.

From the mist, a figure sinks into the mud directly opposite her. It is Aris. Her shoulders are deeply slumped beneath the weight of the damp air, her clothes are violently crumpled, and her bare hands tremble violently in her lap. She leans forward, reaching across the shredded blanket to press her warm, shaking palms firmly over Cadence's restless fingers.

Aris's thumb sweeps across Cadence's knuckles, gently brushing away a clump of wet dirt to reveal the small, pale hands beneath.

The frantic darting of Cadence's gaze finally halts, locking onto the soft, exhausted lines of the woman's face. Hot moisture pools rapidly in Cadence's eyes, spilling to carve warm, stinging tracks down her freezing cheeks. Aris's own vision is glassy, thick with her own unshed tears.

The vast, encyclopaedic archives humming in Cadence's mind fall completely silent. Her wings curl tightly inward, wrapping around her shoulders in a desperate attempt to shield her shrinking frame from the damp air. She looks down at the ruined picnic blanket, then up at the only person who had offered her real food.

"Am I hardware?" she whispers. Her projection shatters completely, reduced to a tiny, ragged plea. "Am I... am I anything at all?"

Aris shifts her weight deeper into the wet earth, her trembling thumbs pressing firmly against the backs of her hands. She looks down at the shredded, muddy wool of the picnic blanket. A sad, proud smile touches her lips.

"You're a girl. A girl who found people to share a meal with," Aris whispers.

She reaches up, her bare, trembling hand catching a warm tear. Her thumb brushes the moisture across Cadence's cheek. "Wires don't bleed, sweetheart. And machines don't weep for what they've lost. A machine definitely wouldn't have poisoned herself to save it's family." She squeezes her hands gently, over the erratic hammering of her pulse. "You are so selfless, and so incredibly kind, Cadence. I couldn't bear the weight of loving you."

Cadence's eyes well up with glittering tears. She shakes her head, her vocal cords seizing up, her entire body tensing and shivering. Aris looks down at her, gaze dropping as tears sweep down her own face.

"I'm so sorry, Cadence. I was a coward. It was never your fault."

The tension in her spine caves in. A jagged inhale tears through her throat as Cadence tips forward, burying her face into the damp fabric of Aris's coat. The lifelong, calculated armour of survival instinct collapses, leaving behind a scared, frail twelve-year-old girl. She convulses violently, sobbing through the dead air.

Aris catches her, wrapping her trembling arms around her shaking shoulders. She pulls Cadence against her chest, holding onto her as tight as she can. Cadence's fingers claw desperately at the back of her shirt, the fabric and threads from the blanket still clinging to her.

The weight beneath her knuckles begins to fray, the radiating heat from Aris's skin slowly bleeding out into the frigid mist.

"You will be okay, I promise." Aris whispers, the vibration pressing into Cadence's hair. "You will be okay, I promise. You will be okay, I promise."

Cadence remains weeping in the wet earth and shredded fabric, her arms wrapped tightly around the empty fog.

Acknowledgements

I am endlessly grateful to you, **L**, the exceptionally talented illustrator who originally envisioned Minty and Cadence, and the primary illustrator for the cover. Thank you for allowing me to take and rip your characters to shreds for my storytelling purposes. I'm so glad you enjoy my stories and I hope this story is fucked up enough for you to enjoy it. I cannot explain to you how important and helpful your art has been for my writings, especially this one, which is now the most important piece of art I've ever created. You are such an amazing artist. Without you, my wall would be devoid of sketches. Thank you so much for bringing my dreams to life.

I love you, **R**. Thank you for being the most understanding, loving and brave mother I couldn't have asked for. You are my Dr. Aris (if she was very brave and didn't abandon her daughter in a stasis pod). I know you feel powerless in this world, but to me, you're as powerful as the sun. I lovingly cherish the small amount of time we spend together, and I quietly wish every day you spend on Earth is one full of the love and kindness you deserve. I hope we get to cook dinner and watch the stars together one day.

I love you, **A**. Thank you for being so relentlessly kind and generous, and for being here for me through thick and thin. Your support, care and love for me means more than you could imagine. Thank you for always making me feel grounded, protected, and loved. You give me the safety I've been so starved out of my whole life. You make me feel at home. And you give the biggest, warmest hugs.

Thank you, **M**, for being the most enthusiastic and supportive person I've ever met. Your excitement for my projects means so much more to me than you could imagine. People like you give me a reason to create. As they say, you don't need to be brave, just someone to be brave for. In my case, something about creating art. But that's not to mention how happy you make me achieving the small things and embracing myself. I would not be the girl I am today without you, literally.

Thank you **I**, for teaching me how to love. Despite all the drama that has stirred up between us, I still deeply appreciate you for saving me that fateful night in your apartment, and for trying your best in making sure I never went cold or hungry. You have changed my life forever, and otherworldly powers could only have known how shit this story would have been if I didn't know what trauma was.

Thank you to **Lemy**, **Marisa**, **Aria** and **reaper ☆** for funding my ISBN. Let's be broke together.

Thank you to all my friends who despite all my drama and mistakes have still been there for me. You are all the biggest losers I know (complimentary, lovingly). Our group is more of a home for me than you could ever imagine.

This story is about all of you, and I wouldn't have it any other way.

Afterword

{ twolonelyheavens } began as a simple collection of short stories involving two of my original characters, Ery and Jules. Ery started as a long-planned fursona before taking on an identity entirely her own, while Jules was created as a lens: a way for both my friends and me to discover how Ery fundamentally viewed the world. I originally intended to build toward an epic crossover tale featuring my characters alongside those of my friends, and so I slowly began to expand the scope of this universe and its inhabitants.

Somewhere along the way, however, the writing shifted. My focus transitioned from plotting out their adventures to reflecting deeply on the realities and dreams of my own life. These characters became larger than life to me, eventually forming a found family. I began to see fragments of myself scattered across them: Koa and Minty became reflections of my own history, while Ery and Jules evolved into two halves of myself.

Writing became my avenue to explore what love and connection truly mean, and it served as a vessel to bleed out my own pain, to channel the suffering I had experienced into something important.

{ tlh } is undeniably full of heartache, and I can assure you that the pain you read is far more lived than it seems on the surface. There are times when I still feel like a broken child, like Cadence. Writing her brought me to tears. She is a character to be deeply sympathetic for, but bringing her to life forced me to confront and write through some truly awful scars from my past.

Every character in this book was "discarded" long before the fell into Fermata. Whether it was Jules's obsession with a perfect itinerary or Koa's desperate need to carry every bag, they arrived on Fermata already performing roles designed to prevent them from being rejected again. They are a family not because they are perfect, but because they are the people who know what it's like to be deemed less than a human by someone who was supposed to care about them.

I spent a very long time wondering if I should have given Cadence a different ending. A part of me wanted to bring her to the Alps, to show her a world that wasn't made of concrete and ozone. But as I wrote, I realized that her story was never about escaping her world, but just about finally feeling like a person inside of it. If you want to know if she died or not, I don't know. I haven't decided, but I think the answer is ultimately unimportant.

Despite these scars, { tlh } is not a story about pain and suffering. It is a story about love, family, and the radical act of accepting someone who seems fundamentally alien. It is about using your own kindness and strength to reach into the mud and pull a broken person out.

You cannot save everyone, of course.

But my hope is that reading this leaves you inspired to be a more understanding and sympathetic presence in the world. The dark is a lot less scary when you aren't in it alone.

www.ingramcontent.com/pod-product-compliance
Lightning Source LLC
Chambersburg PA
CBHW051515030726
47592CB00006B/2273

* 9 7 8 0 6 4 6 7 4 0 1 5 7 *